45145"

The Deeper, The Bluer

◆

The Deeper, The Bluer

◆

Barbara Field

iUniverse.com, Inc.
San Jose New York Lincoln Shanghai

The Deeper, The Bluer

All Rights Reserved © 2000 by Barbara Field

No part of this book may be reproduced or transmitted in any form or by any means, graphic, electronic, or mechanical, including photocopying, recording, taping, or by any information storage retrieval system, without the permission in writing from the publisher.

Published by iUniverse.com, Inc.

For information address:
iUniverse.com, Inc.
5220 S 16th, Ste. 200
Lincoln, NE 68512
www.iuniverse.com

ISBN: 0-595-13378-9

Printed in the United States of America

Dedication

For single mothers who do the best they can,
For my friends who were there time and again,
For my son, Adam, who taught me the power of men,
For my sisters, Phyl and Risa, who helped me get up again,
For my parents, Jean and Richard, who gave me everything.

This book is for you…

Acknowledgments

◆

With deep gratitude to my agents, Jane Dystel and Miriam Goderich, for your faith in me, to Lisa Peters for your talent and beautiful book cover, Michael Farmer (Harcourt Brace) for your ethics and inspiration, Deanne Kells, for editing this and teaching me what real friends are, Nora Cohen for every step of the way (with kisses), Julie Bubar for your photos and creativity, Alice McDermott for your wonderful talent and support, for Alan Zweibel (Castle Rock) for being a mensch and always following through, for Kenzi, Steven, Dana and Valerie (iuniverse) for making this book come to be.

For my best friends with love: Ross Tappen, Philippe Cheng, Pam Barton, Mathew Price, Siggy & Pichie, Bryna Kranzler, Ruthi Warburg, Flora Flam, and Val Estess, Jeanne Conte and Cynthia Williamson (the CBS women)

For your contributions to the book with heartfelt appreciation: Susann Cokal, Diane Drake, Bob Conte & Susie Israelson (HBO), Paige Smith, Sandy, Rita, Ri & Laura, Ivan, Orly Light, Michel Benaroch, Andre Bernard in NY, Carolyn Pearson, Mike Sirota, Deb in Cincinnati, Julie Freeman, Adam Aariely, BJ Brown, Chrissy & Stephanie Poleski, Taryn Bernstein, Jenay Karlson, Christopher Nicolaou, Daniela Mizrahi, Marnie Dilling, Geoff Pope, Ryan McFarland, Dean Berenz, Debbie Breen, Alicia Yaffee, Catie & Emma Huneke, Bill Goldstein

For your intelligence, artistry and inspiration: Joan & Greg Dawson (NBC News-SD), Susan Katz (Showtime), Matthew Eisen (PBS) & Karla Peterson (Union-Tribune), Wendy Haskett, Sara Lewis, Tim Kelleher, Joan Roth, Todd & Adrienne Sharp, Sophia, Richard Walter (UCLA), Debbie Fleming Caffery

For your friendship, generosity and encouragement: Alison & Ron Bendelstein, Orly & Cyril, Flavio, Subhash, Udi, Ruby & my Scripps friends, Camille Wood, Alice A., Dominique Baton in Paris, Zuckie, my Harcourt friends, Sharon & Jason, Stan & Miriam, Sophia & Pat, Diane Demeter, Deb Davidson, Emily Einhorn, The Fields, Barbara Feldman, Uncle Willie & Trudie, Gene Genazzi in Switzerland, Robert Goldstein, Joan & Brent Jacobs, Dr. Thomas & Ann Key, The Korematsus, Andy Katz, Nancy Held Loucas, Tim Langford (Fox News-LA), Sue Maushart (Australia), Pat Magida, Marianne M., Bill Rothbard, Howard Stroll, Elyse Silverberg (Beijing), Andrea, Diane & Joe, Marianna from Bulgaria, Carmen, Mark Wishner, Karen & Carl, Phyllis Q. Steinberg, Sara & Julie, James & Daisy, Audrey & Tamara, Ginita Wall, Pamela H., Mary Ann McGeath, the CV Library staff, WW friends, SDJA friends (especially, Marna, Mike K., the Franks, the Hersch's, Schenks, Essakows, Kaftels, Spunts, Pardos, Braus and Robyn C.) and the Lawrence Family JCC (special thanks to Michael, Marcia, Sandy, Alma, Bernice, Judy and Nathalia, Jackie, Matt, Ana & Sara, Donna & Christine)

Contents

Act I (April & May)

Somewhere Waiting For You (Prologue) 3

The Color of Nothing (Claire) 5

Take Away This Bitter Herb (Dorie) 10

The Belly of a Woman (Renata) 24

The Dream of the Love that Lasts (Molly) 33

Hearts (Claire) 42

Hotter'n a Cowboy's Pistol (Virginia) 48

Like Water (Claire) 53

Courage (Claire) 60

Act II (June & July)

White Nightgowns (Renata) 73

The Pool (Dorie) 85

Reaching and Extension Assists (Molly) 96

The Red Trolley (Virginia) 107

The Lounge Chair (Molly) 111

The Good Hearts and the Old Clocks (Renata) 115

The 21-Piece Comet Band (Claire) 123

Destiny (Claire) 128

Act III (August)

Feeding the Ducks (Renata) *153*

The Best Thing Off the Menu (Claire) *157*

Blue Angels (Claire) *164*

Scrabble and Prayer (Molly) *169*

Embers in the Dark (Claire) *175*

Remember Where the Trees (Virginia) *179*

Cathedrals in Time (Renata) *184*

A Kiss Good-night (Claire) *189*

"We have a beautiful
mother
Her green lap
Immense
Her brown embrace
eternal
Her blue body
everything
we know."

—Alice Walker

"Being human cannot be borne alone. We need other presences. We need soft night noises—a mother speaking downstairs. …We need the little clicks and sighs of a sustaining otherness. We need the gods."

—John Updike

ACT I

(April & May)

Somewhere Waiting For You (Prologue)

♦

Did you ever think that somewhere waiting for you was something important, maybe amazing?

Dorie Lerner waited in platform heels and hipness. She waited for support checks to come regular. She waited for the rain, for wetness. To feel something, anything. And somewhere waiting for her and her two girls in ribbons and daisies was a way out, a way to go on, even though your life wasn't supposed to be like this. She waited for it all to be like news—groundbreaking, immediate, stripped bare. She wanted to be a hotshot reporter and her story to have the speed of a 4-valve V-8 with 305 horsepower on a highway through the desert. She was from LA.

Renata Meyers waited for her handsome husband to catch up to her, waited for what could be virtue, a new spirit or a new architecture. Something real behind the elegance. She waited to make partner, waited for the nanny who was 20 minutes late, waited for the Lexus in the shop. She waited for an eventual return to whiteness. She was like Jackie Kennedy-tough.

Molly Wright waited for the tea hissing from the kettle, for the first whiff of baked bread coming out like steam, for the grab of the Saturday night special clicking in the dark. Molly waited with the fixed face of her pioneering Irish great-grandmother, hands ready to work, her dreams overtaken by Yeats. She'd wear a jean skirt, muted colors and at night maybe a sweater with tiny pearl buttons. And even though her heart wasn't on her sleeve, that's where it would end up.

Virginia waited for her husband to explain how he could ditch her for an actor on a cheesy cop show and leave her to die. She waited to pop caramels when nobody in Ralphs was looking, smearing her lipstick, licking that brown sugary taste. And while she was waiting she figured she might just as well live like hell. So she wore perfume on the treadmill and almost gagged the women in the work out room. She got experimental, illegal drugs from down in Mexico and she loved Claire in a southern accent and too bright colors. "That card," as Dorie called her mama, Claire's mama, Virginia Graham.

And Claire waited for science lab and music practice. She waited for biology and dissecting frogs when they'd leave the scrawny things splat on the teachers' car windshields. Then in the afternoon, she on clarinet, Noah Wright making that tenor sax wail like desire, the clouds out the window carried them. Their reeds vibrated through hollow tubes and out flaring bells into a field of the future, not the real field in which they partied from a keg and puked behind the bushes on their shoes. And after reading The Great Gatsby for dumb English, Claire waited for her own place in the world and she sure as heck hoped it wasn't sitting where the losers sit.

While somewhere waiting for Claire was the summer she would spend with these women in San Diego, four corners of light around an intense square of blue. The summer she prepared to become a mother, not even 17 years old or ready.

And waiting for her was the responsibility of her own life. It was like gravity pulling her down from the heavens to earth and then she found the true center; it wasn't earth at all.

In that pool, around that pool, this pool of women, she learned how to swim passionately, calmly, forcefully, buoyantly—through water.

And everything gave way.

The Color of Nothing (Claire)

◆

"Look at this, Claire," her mama said. "Yes, slap him side the head, Duran. Go, go—" Another boxing match on while outside it was a sunny, spring day.

"Knock Barkley out!" Virginia yelled as Claire entered the smoke-filled den. "Put him down, baby. Now, now. He's soakin up some punishment."

"It's so violent," Claire said, shutting off the TV. "What crap."

Claire breathed smoke. Smoke in her nose, smoke in her head. Smoke inhabited her sharply, like longing. She told Noah there's even smoke in her soul. She lived in a smoky house and she was choking.

Mama lurched to put the TV back on and told the guy flat on his back, "If you can look up, you can get up. Come on—get up, Duran, get up."

"Mama, let's go."

Virginia stood by the set, about to shut it off, but hesitating to watch one more second as Duran rose to his feet. She had seen this old 1989 fight a dozen times. The TV went black. An unlit cigarette dangled from her lips. Her eyes were as blue as pools.

By the door, she stopped to cup Claire's chin in her hand. "Your face is so long. Puff up your cheeks a little, Claire. Can you puff 'em up like this?"

Virginia looked like a blowfish trying to make Claire understand beauty. Claire refused. "Come on, Mama."

"OK, what's your hurry? You got yourself a clear path now. I'm gettin my keys. Now, what did I do with my keys?" She coughed roughly, like an old fisherman.

Last night Claire dreamed she had a snowmachine that looked like a cheese grater. Mama was asleep on the sofa and Claire stood behind her rubbing a snowball over her head so the shredded flakes glistened on her face, her shoulders, bits of white everywhere. Making no clear path to anywhere.

As they walked into Pay-Less, Virginia started. "What is that—neuter color?"

Claire looked at her ivory tee shirt. "It's tasteful."

"Beige is having taste?"

"It's creamy ivory," Claire said, trying to sound like one of those teen magazines Virginia was always trying to get her to read instead of something scientific, something with value.

"It's the color of nothing."

"Well, I'm a nothing."

She let the door almost slam into Claire's face, she was that mad.

"You're a fly girl, Claire, and fly girls always fly high. Remember that."

Claire headed straight to the contraceptive aisle, unafraid. She checked out some different styles of rubbers—Lydia Erikkson always asking Monday morning, "Did anyone bring home a love glove?" As if a rubber was a souvenir. She was a blabbermouth all right. But Claire wasn't after protection or any stupid mitten.

Where did they shelve them? Claire went to the feminine needs aisle. She didn't know women had so many feminine needs. You'd think that after 16 years of life on this planet she'd have a clue. Then she found them. The tests.

Mama turned the corner fast. Claire could sense her a few seconds before, like electricity gone on and she knows how when the storm is approaching to let it bellow, rip the place to bits, let it gush out and blow over. *Then* you pick up the pieces. That's the way you had to handle her mother.

"Use your own money today," Virginia huffed. "I still got to pick my lucky numbers. Be by the car in ten minutes." She was gone just like that.

Claire didn't know why Virginia was mad. She hugged her kit to her like a sacred box—she saw? Maybe not. They could talk sex, drugs, just about anything. But they respected each other too much to talk about things that hurt.

"Hey, stranger." Dorie was in her mid-20s, wore a baseball cap, a mini-dress and platform heels. Claire'd never wear any shoes with a tilt. Dorie's adorable girls, Olivia and Natalie, were hanging on her like branches of a tree.

An ant crossed Dorie's path. "Die, sucker," she said as she gleefully stomped its brains out.

"So when can I baby-sit again?" Claire asked. "Hi, Livie. Natalie, what pretty bracelets." They were one plastic slinky in colors of the rainbow. Natalie clinged shyly. Olivia repeated, "Die, suckah," and stamped her foot.

"Well, I've got a blind date Saturday night. My friend swears he's great. Can you come at 5:30? If it sucks, I'll be home right after we eat."

Dorie was an LA blonde, kind of ditzy.

"Yeah, great. I'll give them their bath, too," Claire volunteered.

"Sucks his thumb?" asked Olivia with a 5-year-old's giggle. Dorie ignored her.

"Would you? Wow, extra time to dress," Dorie smiled.

"Mom, I want a puzzle," Olivia commanded.

"No, sweetie. Daddy hasn't given us any money this month. Where's Natalie?" Dorie's shoes made little squeaks like they were new as she walked away, but Claire knew it just meant they were cheap. She knew from experience.

Claire forgot all about the box and the striped line meaning positive and clear space meaning negative and false positives and positive negatives and all the good and all the bad mixed together. Sex was simply a mixing of body fluids. It was an experiment to see how far a feeling could go, to see what the big deal was.

OK, so she didn't bring home the love glove. Maybe she brought home something better.

Claire paid and passed her mama on the next checkout line. Mama said they were one paycheck away from the streets, but she kept spending. Her stack of greeting cards rode the black conveyor. *What was she wasting her money on cards for?*

"You're late," Claire said casually. Claire was punctual.

"You're not my keeper," Mama growled. "I'll be by the car."

Mama's car was lodged in the handicapped spot. Claire leaned against it, waiting.

A lady came out cupping the back of her newborn's bald head. It looked so soft. Maybe a baby wouldn't be so bad after all. Maybe somewhere waiting for her was a baby. Babies always love you.

Mama looked at the handicapped sign, then at Claire.

"If I'm not handicapped, I don't know who is," Virginia said, fumbling with her keys as her Clairol fell out of the bag.

"Since when do you dye your hair?" Claire read the box.

"First time." They got in.

Mama signaled with the automatic and stuck her arm out the window, going left.

"I'm always honest with you, aren't I?" she asked.

"Of course," Claire said, bored.

"What did you buy?"

"Oh, Trojans, a fifth of Jack Daniels, killer red polish, the usual," Claire flipped.

"That's my baby," she said.

San Diego's sky was dusky blue, and a chorus of lights twinkled on. The palm trees looked fake like in a postcard. Mama announced her teeth were getting whiter. "They added formaldehyde to Crest toothpaste," she said.

"I don't think so," Claire said, elbow out the window. And she opened her mouth to drink in the wind.

That night after she could hear Mama snore, Claire popped a motivational tape in the cassette player in her room. Tony Robbins said, "To develop achievable outcomes, state positively what you want, be specific (how does it look, sound, smell?) and experience the result daily."

I want someone to stay, Claire thought.

She locked the bathroom door and read her box. Over 99% accurate. She wasn't 17 yet, but she knew she could handle things. She was mature.

When she came out, she couldn't stop crying. She ate some ice cream.

Then she sneaked into her mama's room on tiptoe, put the mike near her head and recorded her snore.

Take Away This Bitter Herb (Dorie)

◆

When Dorie last saw them arguing near the stationery aisle in the drugstore, Virginia complained that the cough meant she was dying. Claire was sick of it. She said, "Just trust me, will you? I know science." Dorie had to chase down Natalie and didn't hear the rest. Oh—and she also had to tell the clerk what he could do with himself. He had an attitude problem, that one.

Claire was wise beyond her 16 years, like an old soul who does yoga and just knows things. Claire was even taller than Dorie! And what a baby-sitter. Tonight, when Dorie left, Claire was playing sax for the girls. Like, how cool is that?

Dorie returned, unlocked the door, kicked off her platform shoes. "I'm back early. He was a nerd," she announced.

Claire, smiley and independent, came out from the kitchen.

"Didn't Noah stay tonight?" Dorie asked.

Claire said, "He left earlier. The girls were great; they're sleeping beauties."

Dorie looked around. "Aw. Too bad he's not here."

Then Claire asked, "What is it like to, you know, have them?"

"Give birth?"

"Yeah."

Dorie said agony but amazing agony.

When you started to push your dough-covered face and blanched body out, Livie, you were the reward. And no matter how much I brown puked, how I bore down and believed you'd suck every organ out of me, you didn't leave me empty.

You wrangled and squiggled and escaped like a calf—spurred to life on the day you were expected, the third push after the Epidural the charm. You heaved out as if to say "ready," sculpted in clods of clay, bent legs kicking, arms fisted—followed by a steaky placenta and this was where you came from.

The wettest love in the universe.

That's what she should've told Claire, thought Dorie hours later as she watched her girls sleep. But how do you say that? *Oh Livie, you railed against the dark confines then and now, the way I fight the idea that love goes dry.*

Claire had oohed over the childbirth photos in the gilded album, but she probably wanted to hop a bus. Screw it. Dorie returned the album to the shelf, blood and guts neatly put aside. Photos nobody would cherish but Dorie because most people didn't like seeing things rough and unclean. Come to think of it, there wasn't much blood during the birth. Livie looked like a pasty angel with blue veins. True, the photos weren't the cutesy snapshots that are magnetized to a fridge, but Dorie had no time for glossy fantasy.

You made me a mother, Livie, and hot-damn, I'm gonna remember that every day of my life.

Dorie had flicked on the radio in the living room and leafed through a French *Vogue*. "Don't go yet, Claire, " she had said. "What about my hair—I want to go platinum."

"How was the big date?" Claire asked. Claire grabbed some chips and looked like a teenager.

"My friend Alexxa set me up with a loser who drove a Porsche 911. An impressive looking older guy in his 30s, hard body and sexy. Well, he leaned over his pasta and said, 'Dorie, I want my life to be a celebration.' He looked like Dan Quayle."

Claire laughed. She picked up a *Rolling Stone*.

Dorie continued, "So I said, 'Great.' Then he asked, 'And you?' I go, 'I'm just trying to survive.' We were at an Italian place and he asked if I had any hobbies, if I liked to ski. God, he didn't get it: two kids, no money, single mom. 'I'm not complaining,' I said as I bit into that fresh, warm bread. 'It's just my life.'"

Claire said, "Well, the girls were fine. Natalie was cute. She told me black and white cows make chocolate milk."

"Sweet Natalie."

"I have to go. I hear my mama's crapola car."

"She still won't let you drive?"

"Virginia? Actually trust me? No way."

"Oh—this is U2." Dorie sang, "You give yourself away." Dorie turned up the volume. "Before I dated Paul, I dated a rock-and-roller. He even made a demo. Some demos lead to big record deals and gigs on MTV. My man got a meeting with Bargain Guy Pest Control."

Dorie tipped Claire an extra five bucks and they said good-night. After Claire left, it became too quiet. Dorie turned on the TV, but was that Olivia, her Livie, coughing? She implanted herself on Livie's bed.

When you were three months old, during a blaring cotton July, I was typing, answering "Coldwell Banker, may I help you?" and looking at the rudder of a calendar's boat in a panelled, particle-board office wishing I could be with you. Sometimes the thought of you, Livie, would well in my breasts and I didn't know if this was losing control or just being a mother.

Man, everything in that office smelled like plastic and new machine. You were in daycare at Lenora's in Pacific Beach—that was before I realized she was slugging Scotch in grape jelly glasses— and your father was in Orange County, learning how to leave me. I was suffocating in the dry, hollowed out space.

What happened to the deep-kisses in the dark with the man who gave you life? Where was the slipperiness of birth and sex, the spill of feeling? Daddy and I fought. That's putting it mildly. Cardboard nights we were stiff, mornings flamed with argument. Daddy said, "Dorie, we need your income to pay the rent." I wanted a little pink house like in the John Cougar Mellenkamp song, you know? We barely got the rent check together. The breast pump pinched and my milk wouldn't come. Nipples, how could you fail me? Then Daddy's contracting firm was sued by the architect and they in turn sued the subcontractors. Talk about a man bowed down with negativity.

You didn't sleep through the night until you were six months old, Livie, and that didn't help things at all.

Paul used to say work was for people who didn't surf. But that changed pretty quick…

"Dorie, come on. I've got that meeting tomorrow. Get her. Shit." Paul the some-time breadwinner slunk under the pillow.

"Hey, I work, too, you know." No sleep for days, yet I was still responsible for the housework, you, everything. I was the one with all the energy we agreed, but that became an excuse. Paul liked that I drove a black Mustang convertible with a V-8 engine, worked hard, and played harder. That quickly became history.

Dorie would take Livie to Windansea Beach where they'd watch the surfers and this restless spirit would surge and she'd want to spring on the board with them. Dorie would imagine mouting Livie on her shoulders and they'd whoop it up, wouldn't they? They'd ride the purest, surest wave clear to the shore if only they had a chance to come on in. The first mom and daughter surfer team, huh? Only how could she hold Livie and balance on the sinuous waves at the same time?

Dorie now sat on the bed of her little sassy girl. With her auburn hair and freckles, Livie had her spirit, and Dorie knew if she looked at her too long, she'd sense it somehow and wake. Livie would leave sleep exactly as Dorie did: jolted, shaken, with the catch of a "hmmmm?" For two optimists, it's as if they expected here comes the bad news for sure.

Natalie's delicate cheek-fuzz was warm to her lips. Natalie was the sweet side of Paul. Claire said they probably had Natalie to quiet the bass that rumbled underneath their marriage. Claire's nuts about music and she's got a point about that subway doomsday idea. But Dorie wouldn't ever form a regret. Natalie was at peace anywhere. She wouldn't wake even if Dorie looked at her all night in her Little Mermaid nightgown.

Dorie surveyed her tiny kitchen in her tiny house on Nautilus Street in the Birdrock area. The house wasn't pink like in Mellenkamp's song, it was dilapidated white, but she planted pink geraniums everywhere she could. The moldings were chipping, it needed a paint job, the grass was overgrown and a rusted Orange Cadillac was parked in front of the house next door. But they were near the water, a few blocks away. If only Dorie had time to swim.

She checked the calendar (already April, 1994) and made the girls' lunches. Tomorrow Natalie would go to Jane Meyers's house for another playdate. Their preschool teacher, Mary-Beth, said Natalie and Jane were inseparable. "Dorie, rumors are flying," she whispered as Dorie gathered up Natalie's flowered knapsack one day. "Your daughter is sleeping with Jane Meyers. Every naptime since Monday."

"Little whore," Dorie joked. The teacher laughed uproariously and yelled to David Stern to get off the tire swing NOW.

Dorie wouldn't joke like that with Jane's mother, Renata Meyers. Let's face it. She was the kind of woman who burps and it comes out in French. The perfect nail woman. Renata worked at a cushy law firm in the Golden Triangle and Dorie hoped Renata would represent her. There was something dignified and arrogant about her. The teachers, the other moms—everyone acknowledged her presence in the room. Something about her beautiful dark hair, her gold chain necklace and little Chanel bag. Her cool poise reminds Dorie of Manhattan and Jackie Kennedy.

Too tired to even open the sofabed, she threw a sheet on top, shut off the light and played Tori Amos low as she sacked out on the Granola bar crumbs and a Happy Meal toy. Then, she found Claire's earring. Claire and Noah must have been fooling around. At least Claire was getting some loving. Tomorrow Dorie had to call Paul yet again. No child support for three or four months. Meanwhile, a spanking new—okay, it's two years old, but he just bought it off the Mossy Nissan lot—— white Sentra is parked in front of his apartment on Turquoise Street. Dorie wouldn't have chosen it (slow acceleration, lazy brakes). Why not the 300ZX if you're getting a Nissan? He says money is tight, but hell, how bad could things be? When she went to the bathroom, she realized she had left the front door wide open.

The next morning, a guy in a Fiesta on La Jolla Village Drive cut her off. Dorie gave him the bird.

In the bright southern California sun, the mothers in their Calvin Klein tee-shirts and linen shorts and strappy sandals lined up outside the community center office holding the camp applications. Jane— the splitting image of Renata, her dark-haired mom—was on the playground slide with Dorie's golden Natalie who insisted on a lavender dress and matching girlie socks.

On the premises of the community center was a preschool and camp, a big pool, a great field. Dorie had to get a scholarship for the girls. She was working her butt off, Paul was living the bachelor's life, what could she do?

Dorie wasn't known to shy away from speaking her mind (Paul called it a verbal sewage spill). So when Renata stood on line behind her and asked how she was doing, Dorie told her Paul owed her $1600 in child support payments, that she was working days at Coldwell Banker and waitressing some nights.

Then she mentioned Paul's new car. "It *is* used, " Dorie added.

Renata tsk, tsked. "He's got money for the car but not the girls…"

Dorie didn't say anything because she grew up in cars. New Yorkers don't appreciate cars like Californians do. Dorie lost her virginity in an L.A. traffic jam, and she appreciated horsepower and speed. Give her the 24-valve twin turbo V6 of a Dodge Stealth or the powerful Supra and she wouldn't throw you out of bed.

Then Renata said, pushing her designer sunglasses up the bridge of her nose, "You wanna hear something amazing? I just did research on this. In 1990 the delinquency rate for used car loans was 3% and for child support 48%"

Dorie wondered, if Paul stopped giving her money, would she turn into a statistic? Life sucked—it was so unfair. Renata said that for men, their cars are their babies. Dorie had to admit she loved her little Mustang, but not nearly as much as her lovelies. When she drove home that day ("I like driving with my top down" squared around her license plate), her blonde hair tossed freely in the wind. She just figured she'd win the lottery or something. As her mother always said, luck seemed to follow her.

It was a Saturday, a crisp April morning. Paul said he'd pick up the girls at 8:30 AM. They had been divorced almost a year. Dorie told him her brother Ian had taken off from his job at La Costa and they were going to Borrego Springs so please don't be late.

Livie was ready, but Natalie needing something to cling to. How did she manage to get a kid so clingy to her "stufted" animals and tea parties, who smelled like watermelon? She and Paul should've taken her to San Juan Capistrano. She reminded them of a swallow or the purple martin of the coastal lowlands with her blue eyes and black lashes like Dorie's.

She and the girls sat on the porch — it was unusually warm, the air smelled like jasmine. He arrived an hour and 45 minutes late. Natalie sucked on a string of hair and kicked at the floorboard. Olivia asked

Dorie why Daddy was late again. He apologized and took the girls. How nice it must be to take the girls once a week, to treat them to ice cream and movies and return them before bath time. How nice it must be to be the Dad.

When Dorie returned to the kitchen, she realized she had left the gas range on.

One night Paul sprawled on the couch reading her term paper; she was attending San Diego State then and Livie was toddling around. Something clicked and flickered. A corner was aflame and the paper blackened. Dorie looked at his neck, the back of his head, and she didn't know if Paul watched the paper burn or the Chargers on the television screen. She jumped up in time to see her paper—-all that hard work—shrivel like a leaf. Paul looked up and said, "He had to clip him on the third down. Jesus Christ." During the commercial, Paul said even more. He said something had to go. She dropped out of State. Ugh, why did she listen to him?

She envisioned the flames of her term paper, her house burning down.

Dorie hadn't been to the desert in ages. As a matter of fact she hadn't left San Diego in over a year. Ian, her older brother, drove while she fiddled with the CD's. "That's all, one day a week? Jesus, he lives in town, you'd think he'd see them more." They had already picked up an apple pie at Dudley's in the small town of Julian. They'd been driving almost two hours.

"He's a selfish prick." Dorie didn't want to discuss it.

"Don't the courts require them to see their kids?" he asked innocently, as he checked his rearview mirror. They were picking up county S-2 which connects Ocotillo with state Route 78 at Scissors Crossing. They were on a straightaway, but banked curves and switchbacks appeared.

"The courts don't force them to see their kids. Are you kidding?" The turnoff ahead showed a spectacular view: rocky mountains, valleys at your feet. "Ian, most men are shits after a divorce. They all stop paying their support. It's a fact."

Dorie didn't want to be bitter. She worked days as a receptionist at Coldwell Banker, two nights a week at the Pannikin serving sandwiches, salads, espressos and decaf lattes. Paul had been doing contract jobs here and there. The economy in San Diego was bad. She looked at her nails and remembered polishing them Dusty Rose last April before a big office party. She planned to go back to school to finish her college degree. Her dad went to Yale, after all. Most people underestimated Dorie. But when Paul and she broke up, she had no choice but to work. Olivia was four at the time and very upset by their split. Natalie was only two and she'd hug Dorie on the sofa then and cry.

"Incredible, isn't it?" The scenery was inspiring. They wound their way up narrow two-lane roads cut into the mountain.

Ian was her savior, but not her best friend. He baby-sat at the last minute, sometimes with his girlfriend Kate, sometimes alone. One night Olivia smeared chocolate donuts all over the kitchen and Natalie threw a temper tantrum. Dorie handled that OK, but when Natalie woke up at 3:00 AM with a fever and vomited in Dorie's hands, she called Ian. "I didn't know being a mother meant dealing with puke and crying and shitty Pampers every day of your life." Motherhood meant being a cleaning woman. It meant you give and give and keep on giving.

On the other hand, she thought as she spotted the large, white desert primrose, the absent fathers don't know the clinging close of a feverish child. And Paul wouldn't ever know Natalie's clean apple smell after a bath or her giggle at *The Happy Hippopotami* book. Paul wasn't there to sense Olivia's confident hand in his hand the first day of kindergarten or feel how quickly she let go. He's the one missing it.

"Dorie, I just want to tell you that Kate thinks you're amazing and you've done it all by yourself, with barely any money from him, just working all the time. The scumbag could've gotten a regular job by now. You're gonna find yourself some real prince soon. I know it." Her brother, Ian, was always too good looking for his own good. He put on the new Chris Isaaks release and she checked out the sand verbena's clusters of pink and purple, the quiet around these sharp turns, the miles of cholla, creosote and saltbush.

She laughed. "Find a good guy? I've had two dates in a year. He'll have to be in the supermarket, the school or at daycare cause those are the only places I hang out when I'm not working. Pretty exciting life here." The desert was rich and rocky, not as she remembered it. She was only 25 years old.

They got out before Christmas Circle in town to pick up a map and she felt like her 29 year-old brother with his boots and sunglasses was passing her by. His job as an assistant pro at La Costa with lessons on the side, his girlfriend, the cute bungalow they had in Encinitas, money in mutual funds, his brisk walk as if he had some place to go and that's the only way to get there. An eternity had gone by since her separation and divorce from Paul. The vivid red tassels at the ends of the spiny-fingered Ocotillo shrubs seemed almost obscene. She missed being with a guy. She missed being wet.

In a leather shop, she donned a taxi-driver-black-cap and asked the salesguy for leather gloves.

"Sleek leather," she flirted as she slipped them on. She outlined her breasts, waist and hips while admiring herself in the mirror. A true blonde, pert nose, blue eyes almost gray. Still got the shape! The guy behind the counter just about drooled as she handed him back the gloves. Then she returned the cap on top of the salesguy's head. Ian laughed, but the guy remained mesmerized as they went out the door.

A few days later, as she fixed the kids lunch, Natalie told Dorie she had gone to Disneyland with Daddy and Maxi on Saturday.

"Is Maxi a dog?" Dorie asked. She cut the peanut-butter-and-jelly sandwich into the shape of a star.

Natalie giggled, "No."

"A kitty?"

"No, mom…a wady."

Another time, Natalie and Olivia were coloring at the kitchen table. Natalie said, "Daddy and Maxi taked us to the pancake house. I had apwicot siwup." Dorie slammed the frying pan against the counter.

Natalie said, "You get a time-out."

Dorie sat on the kitchen stool and gave herself a time-out, cursing under her breath. "Taking you for pancakes and to Disneyland—that's more fun than paying your darn Blue Cross." The girls looked at her blankly. "Anyway, I'm sure Maxi *is* a dog," she said smugly.

Natalie sulked that night. She was moodier than Olivia. When Dorie set her alarm she thought about marrying again just for more income. Maybe the kind of executive who rollerblades to work in his suit. Who said business had to be boring?

On Friday, Dorie decided to be happy. She took out her spring clothes, vacuumed around the television, and had the girls' breakfasts ready before they awoke. She arranged to take off from work Monday the 11th and take a course on self-esteem at the community college. Actually, Ian paid for it, and her boss at the real estate office was very cool about her taking a personal day because business was so bad anyway.

On Wednesday, she left a message on Paul's machine to remind him about Monday, but he didn't call back. On Saturday, when he picked up the girls he came 35 minutes late. Olivia went back in for her stuffed snake to bring to Daddy's.

Paul said, "Oh, I can't take them Monday after all. I need to switch to Tuesday."

"What do you mean?" Dorie's voice betrayed her anger.

"I can't do it Monday, Dorie. Hey, I'm helping out here. I'll take them Tuesday."

"You're helping out? I already paid for something. Dammit."

Olivia looked up at Dorie. Paul said, "We've got to be flexible. You said that yourself."

"You goddamn son of a bitch." Dorie was so mad she walked away. She carefully shut and locked the door behind her. She even went to the kitchen to check the gas. Then she realized she forgot to say good-bye to the girls.

She took that course on self-esteem and decided she wanted to date again, have hot sex in the dunes at the beach. Dorie's pal Alexxa asked what kind of guy and Dorie told her, "I'm looking for honor, decency and wildness." Alexxa died laughing.

Dorie bought nailpolish and a summer dres she found in the Salvation Army thrift shop for only six bucks. As she was trying on the dress, a scooped-neck, pink and yellow flowered slip of a thing, it suddenly came to her: she didn't need marriage or divorce all over again. She needed to find a way to make money herself. But how?

"Paul had to switch from Saturday to Sunday last week. He's awful busy for a guy who was laid off and has no money," Dorie joked to Claire on the phone as she wiped down the counters.

"Is it hard being a single mother?" Claire asked. Claire was hard to read, but she was definitely curious.

"Are you kidding me or what? I'm broke. I have to go back to court again. It's a mess. What's going on with Noah?" Dorie asked. "Are you guys getting serious?"

"He's a cute guy," Claire laughed.

"I found your earring," Dorie teased. "Ooh la la."

Claire's voice didn't give away anything. "Thanks. It's Talia's. I borrowed those earrings."

"Hey, tomorrow night is our seder. Ya wanna come?"

"Your seder?"

"My mother is as Irish as they get, but my Dad is the Jewish king and for 31years they've had wild seders, inviting neighbors and friends and Ian's friends and cousins. They once invited the guy who sold them their BMW. No shit. Another year we had the ugly lady from the Post Office. Ian called her Mrs. Beetlejuice."

Before the seder, Dorie dressed the girls in bows and spring clothes. Natalie attended a Jewish preschool at the JCC, and talked about baby Moses, the evil Pharoah and the Jewish slaves. Dorie brought a can of macaroons and wrapped it in one of Olivia's kindergarten paintings. At the seders, her father was never disturbed by the kids running around or her mother's same-old stories or the guests' questions.

Her dad was just beginning with the seder plate. "Why is this night different from all other nights? On all other nights, we eat leavened bread; on this night, we eat only Matzo." Her cousin Jeff smiled brightly. Claire said she'd never been to a Jewish thing before. (Claire asked what that Gefilte fish was floating in. Everyone chuckled. Dorie said, "Nobody knows. That's the great mystery of this religion.")

Dorie's Dad asked Dorie to read next, "On all other nights, we eat all kinds of herbs; on this night, we eat mainly bitters." Then Dorie's father dramatically pointed to the maror, the horseradish, and made an exaggerated sour face. The kids laughed. Her cousin Anna who was sensitive and poetic said, "Take away these bitter herbs, the cruel sufferings of our ancestors in Egypt." Ian said in a gospel voice, "Amen brother." Kate said, "And the cruel sufferings of the homeless and those in Bosnia and Rwanda." And everyone murmured agreement. The Sears repairman who had worked on Dorie's parents' washing machine patted the yarmulke on his head and smiled like an idiot.

After dinner, Olivia was happy because she found the Afikomen, the special dessert matzo, in the TV guide where Dorie's father hides it every year. That meant she got the prize. Dorie's parents were drinking wine on the couch, Natalie on her mother's lap, Olivia playing with Kate on the rug, her cousins and strangers milling around. Dorie could swear one of Ian's friends was selling coke in the bathroom. Her father said, "You know the aim of the seder is that each one of us feel as though he or she had personally come out of Egypt, had personally suffered and witnessed this miracle."

Dorie walked into the kitchen. She dumped the bitters, the horseradish, down the garbage disposal. The rent was due in three days and she was short. What could she do now? Olivia—her little Livie—needed an eye test, maybe glasses. Chickenpox was going around Natalie's class. Jane Meyers was home with it today. She wrapped the leftovers and realized she couldn't stop sobbing. She ran the water loudly.

She was blowing her nose when her red-haired, feisty Livie came into the kitchen and looked at her almost like she knew. "Mommy, come on." Funny how in one clear and unexpected moment bitterness no longer seemed an option.

The Belly of a Woman (Renata)

◆

Renata's day was scheduled like clockwork. But Carmella, her live-in, was late returning from Mexico to visit her sister. So, Renata didn't reach court until 10:00 and her case was called on the calendar at 9:30 AM. The judge marked it for inquest and the plaintiff gave his one-sided testimony. God. It was a big case too. Then Renata had to wait for the Lexus in the shop for 45 minutes. It was supposed to take 10. Her afternoon was meeting after meeting. But she arrived at the JCC before daycare closed, the second-to-last mother. Dorie was always the last. There she was.

Dorie yelled a Happy Passover as she slipped out of her Mustang behind Renata. I don't celebrate it anymore, Renata thought. Not since she married Michael. At first, Renata pegged Dorie a blonde bimbo. Now she considered her a bit immature, but smart; a bit too volatile, but quick like mercury. She was intrigued by her new client: her tawny hair, eyes of blue faience and that spunkiness. And of course Dorie's daughter and her daughter were good friends.

That evening, Renata sat sentry on the bed in her new Donna Karan black suit.

"Look at last year's tax return." Michael pulled out papers from the file. "Look at how much we spent on William's karate lessons, here's for Jane's ear infections," he pulled out more papers. "Mortgage, property taxes, La Jolla Country Day for William. Preschool and daycare for Jane, their piano lessons, CompuServe, your car phone... Here's that receipt from the lodge in Sun Valley." He threw the papers at Renata who sat stoically. "I'm doing our return now and the fact is we just can't afford *it*." The bedroom was a mess. This was the night they had to reset the clocks, spring ahead, lose an hour.

"You're talking about a baby, Michael. Not some thing or electronic gadget." Renata would not relent, her stare was piercing and controlled.

"Kids cost money, Renata. Make the appointment and I'll take off work and go with you. I've got to work on the taxes now. It's already April 13th."

"I thought Catholics were against abortion."

Michael sat down next to her and put his arm around her. "We are."

She wouldn't do it for days. They fought; she wouldn't hear of it. Things got bad. Renata stared at the rotten melon in the trash. She would never let him do this to her.

Claire baby-sat when they went out for dinner. "We gotta talk, " Michael had said. Michael managed to get them a table overlooking the ocean. They sat in high-backed chairs. The other diners looked upscale and proper. All props in a magnificently overpriced restaurant. Michael's teeth gleamed like a model's.

"You think this is easy for me?" he asked as he shut the menu. "You getting the salmon or the swordfish? Huh?"

On the way home from the restaurant, as Michael drove, Renata glanced at her watch in the semi-darkness. She had forgotten to set it ahead. Lose an hour. This spring she would lose much more than an hour she thought as the trees whizzed past La Jolla Scenic.

She knew it was a boy, she didn't know how. She was freighted with different emotions: wonder, disappointment, anger, resignation, maternal feelings, desire.

Michael insisted.

Finally, a few days later, on an unbearably beautiful day, she went to the doctor. She complied.

For weeks after, she'd look at the fingers of infants in carriages. She couldn't get away from the babies in magazine ads. And while she bathed William and Jane, she'd focus on their fingers and toes.

That's when she started swimming again. The turquoise pool at the Lawrence Family Jewish Community Center in the morning and her own pool after the children were asleep in the evening.

She could smell the chlorine from the parking lot. She wouldn't miss a day. When she took on something she saw it through to the end. Bullheaded and determined, she forged ahead. She saw Molly's red hair, blazer and jean skirt just as she was about to put her goggles on. "Hi Molly."

"Just watching them practice," Molly said, as she gestured to her son Noah, Claire and some other teenagers on the Ocean Aquatics Team. "Let's meet for coffee sometime."

"I'd love to," Renata told Molly. Molly's son, Noah, looked at Claire before she took her mark. What a look. Renata missed the part of herself that was a teenager visiting New York City's streets, the part of her that let go.

Renata dived in the pool and instead of coming up for air, pushed herself to hold her breath for two laps.

She'd build up again. She was only 37; she could do it. She had been a swim champion. She'd simply drop her daughter, Jane, at the preschool and walk over to the Olympic-sized pool and challenge herself through the coolness.

After her laps, she leaned against the side of the pool to catch her breath. Then she noticed Claire a few feet away. She was about to say hello.

Noah handed Claire the towel. How pure and simple.

"I'm ready to do it," Claire said matter-of-factly. Renata flinched. Then she held on to each word.

Noah, a confident boy with long brown hair and melting eyes said, "Are you sure?"

Claire didn't move. Noah wrapped his towel around her shoulders and brushed her lips tenderly.

"You love me?" Noah asked as he drew her close to him so that their chins were almost one point.

Claire didn't flinch. "I don't know." She smiled.

He kissed her and in one instant, Renata knew things would never be the same.

Renata thought of Claire and Noah the whole freeway ride to work. How they touched. How Claire was like an echo of her younger self. How time like a chiffon scarf slips away.

After her second meeting, Renata quickly skimmed the custody papers on Dorie Lerner's case. "The usual," she told her assistant. "She filed for increased support so the ex automatically wants to up custody time so he doesn't have to pay more. Seems like he's a few months late on support. OK, we need to file the OSC."

Then Renata imagined Claire standing at the pool. She remembered wanting. That kiss was like a Rodin sculpture, like art transcending something. She snapped back to reality and grabbed her pen. She smiled as her cohort Lee Yamanaka walked by. He was everything she respected: educated, refined, fluent in five languages and a scholar of Japanese history.

The crickets filled the night. Michael was usually working late on floating bonds or a merger and acquisition, but tonight he was squeezing the beer can hard, almost violently at the table. He insisted on cheap beers and doing his own taxes because he didn't trust others to get it right. He thought of himself as a regular guy, the guy next door.

The kids were in bed. Renata had rinsed out her wine glass and was wringing out the sponge over the sink wondering how to tell him she was being promoted to junior partner at her firm. But something was off. There was a sudden spell of humidity from Carlsbad to Ocean Beach that left everyone feeling dizzy. She knew him better than anyone, her husband. They had met through friends who thought: both smart, both athletic and both addicted to crossword puzzles. Here's a match. But this year—their seventh year of marriage—their stark differences stood out.

"So, I stayed in her house, instead of a hotel. And I knew you'd be pissed," Michael said almost defensively.

Renata shook her hands free of the water and dried them, her dark hair swept up in the back with a barrette. Then she sat down next to him. She wore the silk kimono he brought back from his business trip to Asia. To my *Bok wang*, the card said. That was *guiding light* in Korean, but how could he remember.

"What are you telling me, Michael?" she challenged.

"I'm telling the truth for God's sakes. I'm laying it on the table. I stayed in her damn house in Oregon instead of the Hilton and we drove the rental car to the lake and had a lunch. Not a picnic. Some Kentucky Fried chicken. We ate it in the car."

The humidity seeped through the screen door. She had been thirsty all day. Renata took out a Diet Coke and sat back down. She rolled the icy can across the back of her neck and shoulders.

"Then we watched some news on CNN. Then we went to bed," he said.

And for a Godawful few minutes Renata could say nothing.

She imagined her husband running his fingers down another woman's back, then turning her around. She could see the other woman's breasts jutting through her black sheer nightgown and then he'd kiss her. And then he'd kiss her neck and then her belly and then he'd sink to his knees and lift the hem.

But was he saying they watched TV and went to bed? Did he flirt and there was something he didn't act on? They both went to bed and called it a night. Or did they both go to bed and call it something else.

She looked at Michael's rough knuckles squeezing the daylights out of the Budweiser. Living had become a huge chore for him. Like taking out the garbage or cleaning the garage. When he knitted his brows, they formed a brown hairy worm. He was clenching his pretty-boy teeth so as not to show anger. And then he got up, pitched the can in the trash saying, "I don't know," and left the kitchen.

That night it rained. Cars whooshed cautiously, almost dreamlike, then disappeared. It usually doesn't rain in San Diego in May. A sprinkle, maybe, but not like this. It rained all night and the doubt soaked her to the bone. She couldn't ask him the question. And she got up, sleepless, dry mouthed.

The kitchen was no longer familiar. Glass jars of pasta and flour and cookies reflected someone else's contentment. Years, like small cracks in the ceiling and the squeaks of a home, seemed deeper and longer and farther behind her. She wondered which was worse: if he had made love to this woman or really wanted to.

At seven in the morning, she noticed their neighbors, the Lehavins', car pull out of the garage and head toward the Y. She and Michael had lived off La Jolla Scenic for about—yes, it was five years now. Then she heard the *drip, drip*. The roof had leaked. Michael left mumbling, See you later, William took the bus to school, Jane rode in a carpool today. But instead of going to work, Renata called in sick.

Jane had left her Barbie and Ken dolls in the hall. Renata picked up the dolls and studied one and then the other. She placed Ken down in Barbie's private area, then made them kiss, kiss, kiss. Then she flung them across the hall. She pitched William's fire engine and racing cars into the toy box—a cardboard box the kids had painted themselves. She straightened the bedrooms, went to Vons and picked up some asparagus, milk, cantaloupe and Beaujolais.

She dumped the barely-filled pail of water and put it back under the leak. The plumber couldn't get there until tomorrow. Then she sorted the whites and threw them into the washer. Usually Carmella did the housekeeping, but by doing these domestic chores again she could feel herself brace, become immutable, take charge.

She took the white load from the dryer while the clothes were still warm. A white towel, a few pairs of her cotton undies, William's sport socks with the navy stripe on top, some tee shirts of hers and Michael's, Jane's white lacy tights… She folded quickly. Until she came to that nightgown from Victoria's Secret. It had been mixed in with the baby clothes pile, on top of the closet for years, and last week she had found it again.

She had bought it especially to wear in the hospital after she delivered Jane.'Her belly still swelled a bit, but how joyous she had been. It was an easy birth compared to William's. Renata's sister said she looked unbelievably radiant. And Michael had surprised her with irises.

Now she slowed, folding the nightgown, putting it away in the drawer. She slowly looked at the pillows on their bed, head to head. She walked into the kitchen and looked around the nurturing place, the center of a woman's home. Then she went back to the bedroom.

She put on a square-necked linen dress that was the color of buttercream and drove to a sports bar in a strip center at first. Then she changed her mind and headed south past Mission Bay's high-rise hotels, kites and company picnics, and ended up parking in an Ace lot downtown near the Gaslamp Quarter. When she got out, she almost headed toward Horton Plaza's pastel colors and flags, its upscale shops and restaurants. She briskly changed direction and entered one of the older bars wedged in between the newer cafes and bistros where she picked up a fisherman.

"You're from the east coast. I can hear it in the way you speak. How wonderful. I was raised in New York."

"No way. Really? Jimmy Bonalucci."

His eyes were cold blue and reminded her of the Atlantic.

"Renata Meyers," she said and she shook his hand. But she didn't let go.

She took him home and he told her about looking for blue marlin with splashers and swimmers. And he talked about Montauk's bars on Long Island. And she spoke of the blessing of the fleet.

Renata said she had gone to Mexico's Coronado Islands and reeled in some yellowtail but that was forever ago. She heard you could catch anything with a Soby or a Martu hook. And she said she remembered fishing with her dad, who packed her two floats, hooks, swivels, sinkers, 30 feet of monoline and a crappie jig and spoon in a miniature plastic tackle box when she was about 7 or 8. And she said she remembered a boyfriend out in Montauk named Jimmy whose fingers smelled like fish and beer and how beautiful and clean the island looked at low gale.

He was 28, good-looking and a total stranger.

"Guess this is what luck is," he said following her up the stairs past the Barbie and Ken on the floor to the bedroom.

Renata could have done this a million times. Maybe in her fantasies she had. And they sweated and they made love with an intensity that surprised her. "You feel so good," he said and she let go, buried under a wetness, in a darkness that was familiar.

He kissed her neck, her breasts, and rested on her belly.

She hungered for more as if she remembered how much she wanted to live, as if she remembered what appetite and sex and living had in common. She remembered the counselor at sleep-away camp, the only Jewish guy with a tattoo, who met her by the lake early in the morning when the grass was wet with dew. She remembered how his thrusts were so deep she'd sing, Maya, maya, maya. And he told her the word for sin in Hebrew meant "to miss the mark." How generous a God we have she said, all of 15 years old. That hunger again now as she wanted to get on with it.

At a few minutes before four in the afternoon, she threw her silk kimono on and watched as he tucked his white tee shirt into his jeans. Had the rain let up? It was so hot, she drew the curtain and opened the window a crack. It was almost like she was outside again looking in. When she turned around, the guy from New Jersey did the strangest thing.

He headed towards her, angrily. He was twirling his gold band round and round on his finger.

"What?" she asked. "What is it?"

He kept walking toward her, frantically rubbing the ring. As he got closer, his expression became accusing and he took her by the shoulders.

She should've run away, but she couldn't.

"I never ran around on Mary before!" He brandished his five fingers, so she could see the ring near her face like a reprimand.

Renata took in his words like a wallop in the stomach. "Hey, I'm married too…"

"Yeah. OK, a little fun. I'm in paradise all right. But baby, I never expected this." He searched her face for a way out.

She was terrified.

The blueness seemed to drop by degrees until his eyes were so icy it was winter again and she was home on Long Island alone on the white sheets.

He continued, "I don't know how to say this nicely. You've got nice legs and a sweet, sweet body, but I never expected to *feel* for you."

In the fogginess of the late afternoon, his gold ring seemed to be burnished—to momentarily glow with a life of its own. And her wedding band, lying on the dresser across the room, gleamed, almost lifted with light, emanating, haunting with some kind of imperfect beauty.

After more kisses and more wetness and more rain, she turned to look at the time. It was four thirty and the sky was streaked peach and violet. She sat up and looked at the dresser so many yards away, facing it squarely like an enemy. The luster of gold was dimmer now and she was relieved. It was a ring. No more, no less. At least, she had that to thank him for. This fisherman from New Jersey.

The Dream of the Love that Lasts (Molly)

◆

The late afternoon quiet fell like sun motes at Evergreen Nursery on Carmel Mountain Road. The unusual May rainstorm had ended. The streets were muddy and everyone was surprised by the return to normalcy. Molly had welcomed the storm because it reminded her of Washington. She loved the air right after the rain.

But it wasn't right to want something so much.

Molly's copper hair glistened and her green eyes took in the earth and the trees and the flowers and the shrubs.

She was in her element. Renata had wanted her gardener to fill in the patio. Molly volunteered to help as she had a bit of a green thumb, so instead of coffee they met here. Molly spotted Renata's long legs escaping from the Lexus. Renata had the grandeur of a redwood and a solid dignity.

Acres and acres of trees and shrubs and fragrant flowers filled the air. They drove through little streets which had names like Cypress and Sycamore and Hibiscus Way. It was like a foreign country.

"I lived at one of those safe houses," Molly said after they had spoken a few minutes.

"I promised I would never let myself dip into that pool of feeling so I starched my speech and wore only baggy pants, formless and sexless. Husbands are a false sense of security, my friend Vale said. Shirley, who cleaned the center in the mornings and was herself a battered wife, wore a button that said, 'Time wounds all heels.'"

"Molly, it must have been hard for you," Renata said. They mounted a steep hill where the name Evergreen was painted into the grass like the Hollywood sign and 15-gallon trees lined the road. A breeze lifted the silence and Molly could see the hills. For a moment, she imagined the splendor of Italy, but then it all came back.

"The center my children and I stayed at in Bellingham, Washington was tidy and sparse. The General Electric clock in the lounge seemed luxurious, it was so large. Some women played Go Fish but I liked poker and staking myself on the edge—a quickened feeling. I could risk everything and still have Vale, Cynthia and the others josh me after I cleaned them out of two or three dollars. My counselor, Pam, sometimes joined us for a game, but usually she was filling out reports and paperwork in her office with the fan on. She taught me, over the course of many sessions, me sitting on that fold-up chair, Pam holding my hand like it was a fragile gardenia, how to put the beatings behind me, take control by focusing on Noah and Mariah and get on with it."

"How did you manage?" Renata was polite.

"You know, her goodness showed me there was goodness left and I could look for that. Days were nasty and the corridors smelled like Pine-Sol. But Noah and Mariah went to school and were happy to come home to a house of women: frying onions in the kitchen, the tinkle of laughter from the lounge, the secure rolling of a dryer that shook everything out clean and fresh, no matter where the clothes had been or what they had seen."

"Molly, when was this?" Renata asked in her lawyer tone.

Everywhere around Molly was life: passion flowers, roses, hibiscus, a riot of color.

"Two years ago. I became an expert, you see. An expert at not showing the blistering hell; it became just a mistake of a bad marriage in a rainy city."

"You survived," Renata said.

"Survival was getting your speech down. I grew a shell. I developed my professional personality like a sturdy umbrella. And Renata, it worked. It protected my life, but the rain always gets in somehow."

A red jeep slowly approached. Sting's "Fields of Grain" wafted through the air for an other-worldly few minutes.

"Molly, I don't know what to say." Renata was analytical, measured.

"Do you know about Washington's programs?" Molly asked.

"I don't think so."

"They help you disappear. They give you phony addresses and then the shelters help you relocate. But I had to leave the state. So, we opened a map, and Mariah and Noah chose sunny southern California. Noah couldn't believe that even the DMV is peach-colored here. All those tile roofs like we saw in ET. I picked Cardiff-by-the-Sea. I was always a sucker for pretty names."

"Even your children's names are melodic," Renata offered. "Look, if there's some way I can help…"

"I confided in you because last night I felt him."

"Your ex-husband?"

"Sam. Outside my bedroom there was a noise at about four in the morning."

"Were you dreaming maybe?" Renata asked pointedly.

"After so many years of being treated like a dog, the reward is you get their sense. You know the way the air changes…"

"What about a restraining order?"

Everything suddenly seemed hazy. "One for California? Yeah. The old one was just for Washington, I think. Maybe I should look through my papers and make an appointment with you."

Molly's son, Noah, was a wonderful swimmer. A few weeks before, Molly met his girlfriend, Claire. One day, Claire's mother sat next to Molly on the bleachers at one of the kids' swim meets. The meet was six lanes, eighteen kids, 16-18 years old. "This is a 100-yard freestyle. Take your marks." The gun went off. Molly lurched with her whole body and almost toppled off the stand. "You all right, honey?" the woman next to her asked. Noah was in the first heat, doing the freestyle. Claire's mother, Virginia, introduced herself…She smokes like a chimney, but is a pretty southern woman with overstated gestures and a body like a pear.

"Your son, Noah, is a decent boy. Claire's no dullard who turns pink in patches, I'm telling you right here, but she's too serious. He softens her, makes her a girl again. I wish she'd wear more rouge, though." Virginia picked her teeth with the matchbook cover, then giggled. "Gotta pretty up with some lipstick now." She puckered up and applied a garish shade. Molly thought: How nice to be with someone in their 40s like me, who covers the scars.

After the meet, Molly stood within inches of the turquoise edge of the pool. She undid her sandals and put both feet in. The water was freezing. No, not yet. She slipped her sandals on again.

Virginia said, "How'm I gonna fit into my bikini this summer? Renata promised to coach me in swimmin. I can swim a lick. Claire is all over my case about exercise, cuttin down on the cigs. So, you wanna join us? Get sexy for the summer?"

"Maybe," Molly lied. *How long had it been?*

Everything had a rhythm and fell into place until Molly felt him. She confided to a waitress at the Rusty Pelican that she missed being with a man. The words flew out of her mouth like an embarrassment.

"So put on a skirt and get out again." The waitress sported a silver hoop through her tongue and cleared the plates of the handsome biotech managers at the table behind her.

Molly left a tip and caught up with the others from the meeting. But she was distracted at work. She missed her college poetry books and rummaging through fabric stores. She couldn't figure out if she had lost the sense of beauty in her life, trying to be practical and save for the kids. Or if she just needed the rush of an adventure, a little vacation. Or if she needed to feel a man inside her. Pam, her counselor in Bellingham, would say you don't need it, you *want* it.

For three days straight Molly shone her flashlight in corners and checked all the latches on the window screens and the locks on all the doors. She swore the trash can was moved slightly and that the cigarette butts on the grass were his. But there was nothing definite. Renata filed for the restraining order.

A few days later Renata phoned and of all the crazy things, she said she wanted to set Molly up with someone.

"I never do this," she reassured. "I cherish my privacy and I doubt you're into blind dates. It's just that we're on this committee to build a new library downtown and I've known him for awhile."

"I don't know, Renata." Molly tried to sweep the suggestion away. "Thank you for—" It wasn't right to ask for things, but…

"He's charming, head of the dermatology department at Scripps where you work, which made me think of you."

"At Scripps?" Molly brushed her curtains aside and peered out the kitchen window.

"Yes. He's divorced with two grown children in Chicago. It might be nice to have a male friend, get out again." The branches swayed ever so slightly outside Molly's window.

Noah later said Arden rocked Molly's world. But that was later.

Molly waited at the bar at George's. She'd have her glass of red wine, thank him cordially, he is Renata's friend after all, then go home and pop on a Merchant and Ivory video, something with lovely costumes.

She was surprised. He was in his 40s like her, and there was an immediate burning attraction. He had a sharp nose, a rush of brown, sandy hair, and kept in good shape. They had drinks and then dinner and then

browsed through a bookstore. She suggested, "Listen to this," and he said, "You've got to read this:
   I will arise and go now, and go to Innisfree
   And a small cabin build there, of clay and wattles made
   Nine bean-rows will I have there, a hive for the honey-bee,
   And live alone in the bee-loud glade."
   Molly was stunned. Yeats was her favorite poet. And then they poured over photography books in his house and then walked by Powerhouse Park, down the dunes, on the sands of olde Del Mar beach.
   They started seeing each other. Molly took out her dresses from the back of the closet. In the mirror, she eyed a different person. She tried on one dress and was drawn to her bare arms—they looked so vulnerable. But she started to wear dresses again despite her doubts. And he said one day while they sipped iced-teas, "I've watched the way you move and I love the way you walk through the world." She sensed his warmth, his sleeve brushing her skin.
   Their breath got so close she could almost taste his lips. Her eyes closed…she almost let go, she almost slipped—but she pulled away. Just in time.
   And words like beads filled up long necklaces of conversations. She started to see patterns like snowflakes in counter spills and hear musical bells from Africa that filled her chest with contentment. She didn't clean her house for two weeks and remembered what it was like to not just be a mother. He said, "I love the color of your skin."
   She touched her own breasts.
   Sam had never cared about poetry, but he had started with kindnesses. Then the dinner was too cold, whadare ya, stupid? and he'd smack her. Or she didn't follow his directions just right. How many stories she created for the falls, the bruises over the years. And then their car broke down and when he came home he hurled the Colonial lamp at her. Eleven stitches in her forehead. Her mother in her Iowa kitchen didn't believe it. But you have a house, he's a loan officer in a bank.

The day he smashed the kids' hamster against the garage door was the day she knew she'd need help. She tried to leave four times and each time he threatened to beat the crap out of the kids. After he broke Mariah's wrist, she whisked Noah and Mariah to the shelter. Money from AFDC took awhile, but they scrimped. She baked at night and sold her muffins to local bakeries. She got on her feet.

Arden and Molly were leaving the movie theater in the Flower Hill shopping center one night and Arden told her he had memorized her face and body. It was painful. A flash came back to her: seven or eight years ago, Sam and she just finished watching some James Bond movie on TV. Molly felt daring and stripped off her clothes. Sam sat on top of her, looked at her, laughing, and then put his half empty beer can between her breasts.

It was cold. She jerked. The warm beer trickled on the map of her body and all over the sheet. He laughed and said oh man, what a flabby cow. As he turned he let out a huge fart and went downstairs.

But Sam faded and his cruelty grew small and Arden's arm was around her now. She was blocking the memories more quickly. The days and nights spilled together. She glided through the weeks, letting herself out little by little.

Sometimes wanting is stronger than fear.

She finally let Arden kiss her.

One evening, it was a Thursday, Arden's beeper went off again. It was always work or his ex-wife or a woman friend. He came back from the phone and said he was ending a relationship with a woman named Karen that had begun a few weeks before he met Molly. They had been friends for over a year and started something intimate before he met Molly, but now he didn't want it anymore.

When Arden came to pick her up for dinner, she wore her hair in a French twist and he said he so enjoyed seeing her. "Karen was hysterical. I need to get things right by both of you," he confided. Ripples started in

Molly's chest. Sam had once pushed her head underwater in the bathtub while Noah was playing with his trucks in the den and ever since then she had this funny underwater fear.

"Let's talk about it," he said with the full honesty of his blue eyes. They were at a Thai restaurant around the corner from her place and she didn't understand any of the food or how to be with a man in the right way.

"You see me and we try to make this work or that's it," Molly heard herself say.

After Noah went to bed, she cried for the first time in years. She looked in the medicine-cabinet mirror. Nothing swollen. No gashes. Her arms weren't burned by cigarette lances. How could she fall for it again? She couldn't point to the marks, but she couldn't shake off this aching throb, either. Arden said, "Friendship can include tenderness." He had goodness, this man. She respected him for not wanting to hurt that woman at the same time he was hurting her. She opened the screen door from the den and lay down in the wet grass. She cried into the long grass for opening herself to him.

It doesn't feel like over; it doesn't feel it, she thought as she put on her bra and panties this morning. A pit lodged in her stomach. *Maybe his gift wouldn't be like Sam's colognes, lacy teddies on sale, drugstore candy hearts—apologies for almost drowning me and loving me, smashing my fingers with an oar until they were purple and then making love to me the best we ever had it.*

How long would it be until Arden turned meanfisted and masculine? After so many summers in that muddy river called marriage, she'd grown a wilderness in her heart. But her body still retained the impression of oozing mud on her toes, a man's tongue licking her thighs.

Arden didn't call all day at work. It had to be all or nothing.

The kids were by the fence wearing towels around their suits. Molly's car pulled up to the area behind the JCC pool at 5:30 PM. Noah looked nervously at Claire. Claire said, "We don't need to do the one-arm backstroke, 6 strokes right arm and 6 left. What's her problem?"

Noah laughed about the coach. "No wiggle-butt now Claire," he teased, but his eyes looked shyly back at her as he got in the front seat of Molly's car. Claire brushed her lips with a quick raised-shoulder.

"Need a ride?" Molly asked out of her open window.

"Nah. Virginia is coming," Claire said referring to her mother offhandedly. "She's always late."

A crash slowed Molly and Noah down before the 5-805 merge. Noah seemed anxious. Near dinnertime Arden rang the bell. He brought Molly roses that weren't tubular and demure, but voluptuous like chrysanthemums, bursting with life. She readied the iron in her voice. He held her shoulders and said, "I don't just want a relationship with you, a thing, an object. I'm dreaming of a love that lasts."

Noah was in his bedroom, playing a computer game. She thought: It's a shame I can't be swept away anymore, that I wear my mind too tightly. But as he kissed me in the kitchen beside the blue and white curtains, the yellow plates set for Noah and me, I did feel a flutter of a wave, wanting it for always.

Hearts (Claire)

◆

Claire's mama called in sick that day for no reason. Virginia wanted a long Memorial Day weekend. So, she sat in the dark cheering for Kid Ultimate, an amateur champ in the light-middleweight class, as she spit out sunflower seed husks and smoked her brains out.

The purple jacaranda were in bloom and the trees shimmered with a sense of happiness coming soon. School was almost over, the teachers were easing up. The sky was graying and heavy, but you just knew summer was on the tip of your tongue.

Noah's mother, Molly, was at work at Scripps so Claire cut school early and went to Noah's house. She was rocking on clarinet, Noah Wright made that tenor sax wail like desire. The clouds and the wind carried them to a faraway field and their reeds vibrated through hollow tubes out flaring bells into that field of the future.

Talia told Claire that Noah was way cute when a bunch of them went to the movies. Most guys are friendly and like you, then two minutes later they change their minds. Noah wasn't like that, and he didn't get on girls the way some did. He was a jock for sure, but quieter and with longer hair. It was good they went to different high schools. Claire hated all the passing notes and giggling and boyfriend stealing and cattiness at her school.

Molly's kitchen was very clean and had a country feel. Noah handed Claire a can of beer and asked her about her SATs. He said, "My mom keeps pushing me about going away to college, but you can study business anywhere." Noah pulled out a simple ladder-back chair.

"I tell everybody I want to study marine biology just so I have an answer," Claire said, joining him at the table. "I do like dissecting, though."

"I feel like all everyone cares about is college, but what about right now?"

"Yeah."

"Anyway, want to get wasted?"

"Not really," Claire said.

Talia said if you do it once, then he'll know he can get you. "He'll call you late at night for one thing. He'll make the booty call," she warned.

They had had a few Buds and Noah tickled Claire. Then, they kissed. Her body kept wanting him and she was spinning in something new, some indistinct good thing. They carried their instruments into the bedroom. The breeze rippled Molly's curtains. They kissed some more. Noah had on a Laker's cap and unzipped his jeans. He was on top of her. He reached for the table.

"Don't," she said.

"Claire, let me put on a rubber. What's wrong with you?" He was angry and almost grabbed the package.

"Keep going," she kissed him deeply. "Our first time should be special."

"It is special," Noah said.

She said, "Please." She brought his head close to kiss the beer off his lips. Everything seemed a bit muddled. Is this what love is? Swirling skies out the window. Liking everything.

"You're doing this on purpose. It's not feeling, not because you love me."

"We have to do it tonight," Claire said.

Noah said, "We *have* to? You just want to get it over with?"

"No, Noah."

"Then, what is it? What's tonight?"

"It's the right time." She rolled over so she wouldn't have to face him.

Noah said, "Oh. I feel it's right, too." He kissed her hair.

Claire said, "The right time of month. I'm ovulating."

"Shit! You're trying to get goddamn pregnant?" He jumped up and put on the light. He looked at her like she was insane. "Are you nuts?"

Claire answered, "It's your mother's room. This is too weird." The whole house smelled like cinnamon and raspberry pinwheel cookies and fresh bread.

"What does that have to do with anything? Christ, *I'm* begging *you* to let me wear a condom? Something wrong with this picture."

Molly's room was decorated with simplicity. A rocker, natural pine furniture, prints of wildflowers, earthen pottery. A pillow was embroidered with the Shakers' motto: "Hands to work; hearts to God." They had bought the rocker at Ikea and a hutch at a consignment shop.

"What's the story, Claire?" Noah was exasperated.

Claire didn't answer.

"Didn't you have those eggs to take care of in 7th grade?" Noah asked.

"What?"

"In health class. You get the egg, name it, keep it in a foam box for a couple days and pretend it's a baby."

"No, we just talked about anatomy in health."

"Well, I had the egg class. And I dropped my egg. I did. The first night, too. Then I made it into a western omelet. I ate it, Claire!"

There was a moment when neither spoke.

"What a father I'd be, huh?"

"I never told you about my father," Claire said. "It's Memorial Day. We're supposed to remember the dead." She wouldn't look at him. She stayed lying on her side.

"I thought we remember veterans and soldiers."

"He's dead. That's close enough."

"You said he died last fall."

"The day of his funeral, clouds piffled up and looked disgusted like he died of weakness. Mama dressed totally inappropriate in a bright red chiffon mini-thing and I told her my buddy Robbie Kohler got a new telescope and I wanted one. She grabbed me, and said, "Listen, Claire. Robbie wants to be like *you*. He's always wanted to be like you even when he was younger than you years ago."

Claire stopped.

"But he's still younger than me I thought. Duhhh. My mother always spun a twist on things, even at my dad's funeral: she had her friend from the mall come, Mark Ellis, playing the trumpet, because she said Dad liked dramatics. And she called the newspaper to cover the story.

'My husband died of AIDS,' Mama said and the lighter from Las Vegas sent a plume up in the air. She sucked on her Salem Light and spoke into the phone. 'You should take pictures at the funeral because it's families now. You guys are showing gays all the time and those quilts and marches, but what about us families? It's just me and my little girl now.' She covered the holes on the mouthpiece and mouthed to me, 'Cry, come on. Cry.' Then, she got pissed at me when I wouldn't.'"

Noah didn't dare interrupt. This was something important.

"It's not that my mother didn't love my father with her whole heart and being. It's just that she didn't feel she got justice in her world. Here she screwed up for years dating the wrong men, she says, and she finally goes and meets someone wonderful only he's a painter and makes no money, but he's a good man. And now to have him die like an old bag of bones? she asks."

Noah lied back down on the bed. Claire rolled on her back and looked at him. He stared at the ceiling, one arm crooked behind his head.

"When I was 6, we went to the zoo. I watched the spotted giraffe intently because it somehow reminded me of Mama. She stuck her neck out too far, she wore slingback heels to the beach for Godsakes and oh, she talked too much out of place so that my teacher, Mr. Stenner, rolled his eyes the day she came to get me for a dentist appointment. I shrank next to her. My library book said giraffes were afraid of heights. When Mama kissed me good-night, her hair smelled like Herbal Essence, I showed her the part next to the picture about giraffes being afraid to step up or down past six inches and she said they were smart not to risk too much.

"My mother was brave but she didn't know her boundaries. She hadn't studied European painting in a college in Massachusetts like my Dad; she grew up in the South and in Cincinnati where she could smell the brewery every day as she walked to school in Clifton. She doesn't pretend to be anything else but who she is. You know that, Noah. You've seen Virginia Graham in action.

"How many women drive a VW bug with a license plate that says PMS Blus? She is a stickler for safety rules, clicking on her turn signal though no cars are on the road, stopping on the yellow light. Mama is humbled by machines. She hasn't learned to use the dishwasher though we've lived in the house for almost three years. And she never let me plug the radio into the socket near the shower. She offered to sing to me instead.

"At Daddy's funeral, one jerk from the *San Diego Union-Tribune* came, but he never wrote about us. Robbie's father was there, square-jawed and businesslike. The air was gray and October leaves clung to scrawny trees. Mama fiddled with the Scotch tape holding up the hem of her dress. Then, my mother squeezed my hand a few times and at one point she sucked in all her sorrow, bit her lip and looked straight up like an arrow. Her body was so tight in that fluttery red dress and her beautiful neck extended like a giraffe's beyond the area we knew to be safe. She cried and the snot ran out of her nose.

"'Claire,' she barely whispered, jamming her eyes shut so that tears were squeezed out like from a roller. 'Claire,' she said, lowering her head, then crouching, she kneeled down on the ground next to me, her nylon knees in the mud, turning my body to her, 'Oh Claire, honey.' She hugged into my new bra and I felt like a tyrannosaurus with his arms too tiny, too tiny to put around my mother.

"I got into the back seat of the car to get some space.

"I don't know if she knew she was HIV positive the day of my dad's funeral. I do know that on the way home, I unbuckled my seatbelt and it was sucked back into nothingness. My mama's eyes darted from the 5 freeway to the rear-view mirror, back to the northern road, back to me.

"I then heard a hard slap. It was the retraction of her lap belt, the lap belt of a woman who lived for safety rules. I saw the shoulder harness whip back angrily as if nobody was left in the driver's seat. What had she done? My mother's intense blue eyes gazed at me in the rear-view mirror again. We both sat dangerously free, both of us vigilant. My mother and I, the muscle, now the heart of our shrinking family."

Noah hugged Claire as if he could shelter her. He loved the way she never flipped her hair back, but it fell in her eyes all the same. She was tall and smart and she didn't fit in, just like him. They talked some soft talk. Then, they kissed. Actually, they kissed for a long time. The walls were dappled with shadows. She was swirling again.

They did it—mixed the fluids. Claire felt something, but she tried not to. She felt old.

They gathered up their clothes and she could still hear it. That slap of the belt followed her. It seemed to echo in the room all the way from memory to the Wright's house and back again.

Hotter'n a Cowboy's Pistol (Virginia)

♦

"It's hotter'n a cowboy's pistol in here," Virginia told Claire's empty room. Her earrings dangled and her cigarette lighted a path of ash as she made her way in her pink sweatsuit and white Mervyn's pumps toward the window in hopes of getting some fresh air in the place.

Claire's room looks like a Motel 6. I swear, Virginia thought. On her nightstand she had two packages of batteries, on her bureau, her radio and CD player, a few CD's and one picture. A pile of clothes on one chair, a backpack and books on the desk, one painting of bones on the wall. Claire had thrown out her good money on a striped bedspread and outright refused to sleep with that darlin peach comforter abloom with roses. She fought Virginia for days over the pretty lavender curtains. That girl. Claire said she was an earth tones person. Call that color? What kind of 16-year old girl don't like feminine things like a big canopy bed and ruffled curtains from JC Penney's and Siren Red lipstick by Cover Girl like Virginia left on her bureau one day.

Virginia unlatched the lock and opened the window. A box on the sill behind the curtains fell behind the nightstand, but Virginia didn't notice. She was attracted to the framed picture on top of the bureau.

What did you do it for, Vince? Claire and her father smiled from Pt. Loma. They had just spotted California gray whales swimmin to Baja. Lordy, what a waste of a man. You were such a good man, Vince. Now your little girl's got a dead faggot for a daddy.

Claire traipsed in, her hair stringy wet. She wore a big jean jacket that didn't fit her. "Hey, you're not getting soft on me, now?" she said.

Virginia retorted, "You're dumb as a box of rocks." She looked back at the picture.

Claire asked, "Why did I have to look like him, anyway? I could have had your cheekbones and your pretty eyes."

Virginia said, "Well, sweets, I wanted you so crazy, I took to bed. I guess I rested too much. Your daddy's genes swam more powerful than mine."

Claire got the know-it-all tone. "Are you kidding? That's not how it works."

"Course it does. If I was more active them genes of mine woulda raced and won. You coulda got blue eyes. I shoulda focused more on everything blue."

Virginia returned to Claire's face in the photograph. Claire wasn't like one of 'em prom queens. She had natural beauty. A little too tall, but... Some might say she's plain, but she's no vanilla inside. She's smart and grounded.

Claire seemed bored. "I better do my homework."

Virginia continued, "You wouldn't have gotten such a long horsy face. That's from his people."

Claire yelled, "Mama, I gotta do my work."

"Then why you on the phone?"

Claire said, "I have to tell Talia something important."

Virginia said, "You're always on the phone and it seems like nothin worth a titty gets talked about."

Claire was frustrated. "It's still busy."

Virginia said, "What's so important? Come have lemonade with me while I fix you some supper. Come on. Let's you and me get reacquainted." Claire was, after all, her one and only baby girl.

Virginia put two chicken pot pies in the oven and turned the dial to 350. She retrieved the plastic pitcher from behind a Christmas cookies tine and she stood for a moment.

Claire yelled, "I wish she'd get call waiting. Hey, did you listen to those Les Brown and Brian Tracy tapes?" Claire came in and sat down, leaned back and splayed her legs wide like a man would do.

"Aren't you lookin fine, sittin so lady-like! No, I didn't listen to 'em." Virginia looked at the crystal, hanging from the elastic cord around her neck. "But I like this here crystal. It makes a rainbow." The water gushed over the ice chunk of frozen lemonade. "The talking tapes—I don't know. Those fellas ain't keepin me warm in bed at night or fixin this old truck of a body here with words."

Claire argued, "We'll find a way. You're too stubborn to give up." She looked at the crystal she had given her mother the other day.

Virginia said, "Nobody here's givin up. OK, darn. I'll play the tapes, but words can't…I still got to set my dishes in order in case." She took out the silverware as she spoke. "I got to. Every last spoon and fork and knife. If I die, I'm still responsible for you."

Claire said, "I'll read more."

"Just because you read don't make you smart."

Claire banged the table with one fist. "Mama, I'm a big girl and—"

Virginia pointed the knife at Claire. "You think at 16 you have all the answers? Then you *are* dumb as a box of rocks. You think-"

Claire calmly stated, "I'm not listening…"

Virginia was hot now, "If I die, what happens to you, huh? HUH?"

Virginia wiped her hands on the towel with painted cherries and Myrtle Beach printed on it and shook her head obstinately. Fightin was fine, but this was different.

Then Claire stood up and made use of her lungs, "Can't you find one bit of brain power in there? Under all that makeup and all those fancy shmancy outfits and those dangly jewels. Get it into that Virginia

Graham truck of yours! You're HIV positive, Mama—I keep telling you that's different than having AIDS!"

Virginia yelled back, "OK, Miss Smartypants. But let me ask you somethin. Don't one come before the other?"

"Not always!" Claire sat down again, but her face lost its color.

Virginia rubbed her crystal. Maybe a genie would appear and tell her what to do now. Maybe she could make a wish—just one wish. She looked at Claire. Maybe she could conjure the color from the crystal's rainbow to fill out those cheeks of her daughter.

Virginia had to respond fast. Some might call it instinct or intuition or a biological reflex. Virginia knew it as the tearing at her heart. She grabbed for Claire's shoulder. "OK, OK." Virginia shook her daughter as if to wake her from this. "I'm getting better. I'm a POWERFUL ME. Virginia unlimited and ain't no HIV virus gonna stop me. OK?"

Virginia returned to the sink and said, "Get the plates and set the table now. I'm starvin. Let's go." Virginia couldn't abide waiting.

Just keep going. Do right by her.

Virginia felt her daughter's slowness. Her daughter who dragged the weight of worry with her like a heavy-cased black instrument.

"Hurry up now, Claire. I swear you're as slow as molasses."

They didn't need knives. Thank the lord. They had cut up each other enough, Virginia thought. But the chicken pot pie sure did smell good as she put it on the table. She was hungry, come to think of it.

Virginia sipped her lemonade and smacked her lips. "Hmmmm. Better than that other brand's piss water. This is sweet."

"Just like you, Mama."

Virginia figured they were OK. "I got peach pie from Marie Callendars for dessert."

"I like blueberry better."

Virginia said, "Don't be contrary. Now hush up. You love peach pie. But I didn't get no vanilla a la mode on account of I got to lose a few pounds. So don't be askin where's the a la mode? Summer's almost here, you know."

"Bring on the bees," Claire said.

Like Water (Claire)

◆

Renata had money. You could tell. Her house was like a mansion. Even the mauve towels in the bathroom were thick and plush. Claire opened two of them and neither had a single moth hole in them. As she came downstairs after Renata's little girl's birthday party, Claire was thinking what she'd do if Noah didn't care anymore. He was avoiding her. Did they do something dirty? Was it over?

When she thought of that afternoon, she blurred the swirling clouds and the gray clouds of her dad's funeral and the improvised sax that took her down the B flat, D flat blues and how loving was blurry and tasted salty. And how moments could hurt like a sudden F sharp.

A baby would need me, Claire thought. I can feel the softness, smell that clean baby powder smell. Maybe I'd have a quiet little one like Dorie's daughter, Natalie. She baby-sat her girls the other night.

In school, Claire had an algebra test with two questions on parabolas, and this other chick was flirting with Nathan, her best friend's boyfriend. Talia doesn't know. Just because they broke up doesn't mean you just go and get on someone's boyfriend. They might get back together. The girls just backstab each other in high school. Backstab and lie.

On the ride over to Renata's, Mama asked, "That day, you weren't buyin no rubbers at Pay-Less now, were ya?"

"No, Mama," Claire had said.

"You're always honest with me, Claire?" Virginia prodded.

"Of course." She had to stifle a smile. Truth was a strange bugger all right. Funny how by telling the truth she was almost presenting a lie. A lie that sex was not nearby.

Mama's hearty laugh burst from Renata's patio like a firecracker. What was she carrying on about now? As Claire opened the French doors, their voices jingled from the area around the pool. Claire had been playing with the kids upstairs since Jane's party ended hours ago.

Meanwhile, the women out there were getting plastered. The women in that pool, around that pool, this pool of women.

"I'm having my three glasses of water a day," Mama said pouring from the bottle of Tanqueray and laughing. She was holding court. "So didn't you have a say so?" She squinted through her cigarette smoke and waited for Dorie's answer.

"A say so? It's not like this, twisting Oreos," Dorie said, demonstrating. "It's not like evenly divided: he takes the girls, I take the girls. He takes 'em only when it's convenient." She licked the cream. Dorie wore big hoops, white-pink lipstick and her dyed blonde California hair on top of her head like a waterfall. "Pour me a shot, Virginia. Now the fucker wants full custody."

"No way…"

If Dorie played an instrument, it would be a defiant rock-and-roll guitar. What Mama would play, that's easy—something in brass.

Renata, in a navy and white tennis-looking outfit, came out of the palace, watched Dorie play with the cookies and said, "You know, I read somewhere that one out of every three people twist their Oreos like that." Renata's husband, Michael, put his arm around her, chugged down his Corona and teased, "She even knows the weather in Bombay right now."

Renata had that well-bred horse air. She'd play something classical. She'd be a string player because strings can enter on a whisper or a mist.

They can fake it with vibrato, blur the edges. Claire thought her mama could never come on without one big blow of wind.

Virginia and Dorie talked a mile a minute. Meanwhile, Renata, the proper hostess, asked quiet Molly if she wanted anything else to eat. Molly was in love with Arden these days. They had just returned from a weekend in Santa Barbara. She stood up and said, "No. I'll take in Jane's birthday gifts. It was such a sweet party."

She scooped up the gifts and Molly's white cotton blouse and buttercup flowered skirt whooshed by. Molly and Renata's husband, Michael, locked eyes for a moment and then both looked away.

The pool was dazzling blue like it was lit up from underneath.

Claire was almost invisible with her feet dangling in the water. She sucked the ice and kept spitting it back in the paper cup decorated with blue elephants and pink hippos. Let's see, Noah's mother, Molly, is super feminine. She'd play the flute. No—the harp because it sweeps you away.

Would Molly tell Noah she was here tonight? Do they talk like that, mother-to-son? It was nice to get away from the garbage gab at school, from the fake girls. This was real life. These were real mothers. Here Claire got to see what her mother could have been.

Debutante Renata sat down and joined the group. "Dorie, your girls are conked out in sleeping bags. My live-in watches the kids. You didn't need to hire Claire."

"I wanted to come," Claire piped up. That wasn't completely true. Noah hadn't called and she didn't want to be waiting for him.

Dorie answered, "Well, Claire was going to baby-sit for me cause I was supposed to have another loser date. But hell, sitting out here with you guys, on a night like this…"

"It's a beautiful night," Molly said returning to her seat.

Dorie announced, "News flash, everyone." She banged the spoon against the glass. "Renata is my lawyer now; it's official." She raised her glass.

Renata smiled.

"To smart women lawyers," said Mama raising her glass, her nails brightly polished. "You Jews sure got the brains. We need tonic water."

"I'll get it," Michael volunteered. He was cute all right, as far as husbands go.

"And where are them little limes? Let's have a good time." Mama Virginia cleared her throat. "All that whoopin and hollerin today at your little girl's party. I—"

"Sorry they got wild," Renata said as she downed the shot in one gulp. Claire figured she'd be more of the white-wine-sipper type.

"Nothin wrong with that. I like hollerin. Claire and me got a good hollerin home." Mama belched and ,percussioning her breast three times, said in a lady-like tone, "My, my."

"Turn that up," said Dorie, going over to the boom-box herself as En Vogue came on. Dorie and Mama both got up, Dorie in her halter rubber dress and Claire's Virginia in leggings and a fuchsia overblouse.

"Ow."

"Ah right."

"No, you're never gonna get it, not this time, my lovin."

"No, you're never gonna get it.

Sweet lovin."

"Eee-yeah," cried Virginia with her hands up in the air like Zorba the Greek. "Come on, Claire."

"I don't feel like it." The music was great; the dancing part she didn't care for.

Dorie swiveled her hips, shook her breasts provocatively and let loose. Then she grapevined and turned. Dorie sang along, "What makes you think you can walk into her life?" They bumped and grinded and "oh babe-uh"-ed with a vengeance.

Molly and Renata grooved in their seats. They didn't say anything for awhile.

Molly prompted, "Go dance."

"I don't dance," Renata said. Molly wrapped her sweater around her. The tiny pearl buttons shone like globular moons.

The song ended. Mama and Dorie were whispering, giggling. Renata and Molly were more reserved.

Michael returned and set the requested tonic water near Mama's seat and then went over to massage Renata's shoulders. "Where are my Bliss cookies?" he asked.

"They're oatmeal raisin with Macadamia nuts, his favorite," Renata explained to Molly. "I didn't have time this year," Renata directed to Michael. "Michael's and Jane's birthdays are a day apart," she told the air.

"Oh, baby…" Michael sighed and stopped massaging her shoulders. He walked into the house.

Renata stood by the pool. "It's so arbitrary sometimes whether you hold on or let go," she said as her foot skimmed the water.

Nobody answered.

Claire poured more Coke in her cup and wondered what marriage was like. Her daddy was never there long enough. She couldn't imagine Noah as a husband. Here she was, she had her license, being 16 and all, but Mama didn't trust her to drive and they only had one car. So, she was stuck here waiting for her mama to take her home, waiting to get back to her music, waiting to be whoever she was supposed to be.

"Look at how clear it is. Like water," Dorie said returning to her seat, gazing at the gin and gulping it down. She was smackered. "I want to find the Wow in things." She was a bit winded, "I'm looking for the Wow."

Mama plopped into the chair. "The wow? I'm just glad I got my own teeth. Over in Kentucky, half my sister's friends got metal in their mouth. Steel magnolias all right."

Molly hadn't said much until then. "Virginia, I hear your doctors are at Scripps Clinic. I work in communications, second floor, in PR. Next time you're there, why don't you stop by?" She pushed her red bangs off her forehead. Noah had strong features like his mom, but not her airy, dreamy presence. He told Claire his mom baked all night and sold muffins when they lived in Washington.

"Shoot, why not? You got a nice boy, that Noah. Claire's interest in boys wasn't worth a doodle-de-squat until your boy came along."

"Quit it, Mama," Claire said.

"At least *somebody's* in love. Here we are, all of us, single. Single and mothers. Two strikes," said Dorie tapping Virginia's cigarette in the ashtray. Claire thought Dorie wasn't like the sluts at school. Kind of, but Dorie was hipper.

"Single mothers with dirt for pocket change. Three strikes," Mama added with enthusiasm.

Renata stated, "I'm not single." She used a napkin to blot her lipstick.

"Right. And the hard part isn't raising kids alone. It's not having money for your kids," Molly commanded and just like that she drifted into space, probably off into a dream about Arden.

"Well, I think it's the thunder thighs," Virginia announced. "I never saw no stretch marks but after Claire beamed into this world, shoot, my thighs became turkey-sized."

Dorie jumped in. "That can't be the worst part of this motherhood thing."

Mama said, "I ain't sure."

Dorie continued, "After work and the girls, I'm a dishrag. And it's lonely at night. I'd rather feel anything than that." She was a babe—the blue eyes, blonde hair.

"Maybe not," Molly said and smiled too quickly. She started fooling with the flowers in the vase. It got quiet fast. You could hear the cold splashes Claire's legs made as they washed through the water. She was still dangling her feet in the pool, dipping into their conversations.

"Weren't you one of them battery wives?" Mama blurted out. The others tittered.

Molly said, "I'm not part of the battered wives lunch club, but...He's in Seattle or Bellingham. Or at least that's where he's supposed to be.

This is heavenly sitting by the pool." She looked toward the pool—and Claire. The subject was closed and you knew there was firmness under all that dreaminess.

Renata narrowed her eyes like she was studying the situation.

Nobody said anything. Claire realized that kids brought these different women together. Not men, not work. But the men were on their minds.

Dorie said, "I figured out the $200 on my phone bill was charged to a 900 phone sex number." She spinned Mama's ashtray around. "Paul charged those calls from my house after we broke up!"

"Nooo..." Mama's eyes lit up.

Dorie added, "The bill showed calls every minute or two. How could he dial that fast?"

"Why so many?" asked logical Renata.

"Maybe he didn't like what the first one said," Mama chuckled.

Dorie washed a bit of gin into her hair. "Hmmm," she said.

Mama laughed. They both liked anything outrageous.

"A new conditioner?" asked Renata.

"Like my sister's mayonnaise, only this one has a little kick," Mama said.

Dorie poured more in her hair. "It feels good wet."

"You reek. Call it U-reek-a, Eureka Conditioner," Molly added good-naturedly.

Dorie took the bottle and then drenched herself.

Molly cautioned, "Hey, Tanqueray isn't cheap."

"It's okay," said Renata the hostess and she recrossed her legs.

Molly looked longingly at the pool and said, "I'm looking forward to the summer."

Dorie said, "I'm looking forward to getting laid."

Courage (Claire)

◆

"I'm ready for a relationship, but I'm not ready to be devastated by one," said Molly, referring to the Arden-Molly hot topic.

"Oh, I'm ready to be devastated by one," laughed Dorie throatily as she poured the tea. Dorie was just a few years older than Claire, almost half Mama's age. But she seemed screwy and fun enough to be Mama's true daughter.

They sat at Virginia's dinette and pretended they were British ladies biting into ladyfingers at high tea. It was Molly's idea. She made cucumber sandwiches.

You would've never known that Mama had, seven months before, buried her husband of seventeen years weighing all of 82 pounds in a newly dug grave, her husband who had for the three years before his diagnosis been screwing an actor on a cop show in L.A.

Claire remembered it was hard for her dad to get into those clinical trials. When they started administering the AZT and her dad got anemic was when her mother began to read their horoscopes out loud religiously. Claire's an Aquarius, which explains her impatience with the tried-and-true. Her mama is an Aries, so you'd better stay on her good side. But Claire didn't really believe that stuff. She barely listened to those daily forecasts, but they gave her mother comfort.

She started skipping a few nights at the hospital with her dad. Her mama was especially tired. And Claire got boiling angry at her father for doing this to her. Mama said she chose to take the high road and never once talked about the actor with the dimples.

To the ladies in the kitchen, Mama said, "Condoms come in all colors now, ladies." She loved to be outrageous.

"They sure do," Claire said to tease her mother.

Molly looked uncomfortable.

"But you know men, will they wear em? Just because it's right doesn't mean they act on it," Dorie reminded and sipped her tea.

"What d'ya mean?" Claire asked, biting into one of those cream cheese and cucumber sandwiches, then spitting it out in a napkin.

"It's all the same hogwash. They tell you I love you, we don't need protection. I want to have a baby with you right now. Have my baby," Molly imitated in a fake Latin lover voice.

Dorie laughed, "And you fall for that crap?"

"Of course not," Molly said.

"He wanted to see Claire go to some high-falutin east coast music school," Mama's voice faltered.

"Virginia, you OK?" Molly asked.

Mama snapped. "He gave me fucking AIDS and I'm fucking going to die because he fucked a fucking actor. And what about my baby?"

Mama was adamant about clean language in their house and thank goodness she was taking the high road.

"You're HIV positive. You don't have AIDS," Claire corrected.

Dorie patted Virginia's back, reassuring. "I read in the French *Vogue* that paisley is coming back. I thought you should know that." Everyone cracked up.

"Men wear paisley ties because it looks like sperm," Mama remarked, and all three of them laughed as if this truth explained all the heartache in the world.

"I should advertise for a sperm bank. I'm 25. I need some loving," Dorie piped in. She lowered the rattling teacup into the sink.

"Why not do those personals?" Molly suggested, carrying her own cup to the sink. You just knew Molly never would.

"Answer one, you mean, or write your own?" Dorie wanted to know.

Without seeing their expressions, Claire could fill in the lines.

The lighthouse was solitary, steadfast, cold. It was like the single mother guiding her children. Virginia took Claire to Pt. Loma whenever she was feeling twinges of sentimental stuff. They had last gone in January or February, Claire remembered. Dad had painted Mama here, except her body and face were fractured into colors and lines so that all that was left of her mother was the vibrancy of cobalt blue. That was her mama. She'd recognize her anywhere.

They drank hot chocolate and bought plastic placemats. That evening a frilly edge of purple sank into the ocean as they plowed up North Torrey Pines past the Reserve in the red convertible Mazda Miata that Virginia rented for the day. Claire didn't even want to know how much it cost. Mama had a strong nose, dark blowing hair like an Italian's and a crooked smile, neither sincere nor alluring. "I finally feel at peace, Claire."

Claire was having a contact attack. Her left eye was tearing. Little did she know what her mama had in store.

After the tea party and the drive to Point Loma, Virginia wrote until 2 AM. Claire didn't know what the deal was, but her mama's hand shook.

The next day, Talia hugged Claire by her locker. Claire said, "I've got to talk to you. Your line is always busy." But Claire had to wait.

Talia had to report the latest first. Janelle Smythe told Talia's mother that Talia's sister was taking crystal meth to lose weight. Talia's mother was so straight, she didn't even have aspirin in the house and she went crazy hearing this. Talia yelled at her mother, "Don't you take into account where your information is coming from?" Talia's sister, Elizabeth, didn't take hard-core stuff or even diet pills. She didn't need to. Every day after fifth period, on a regular basis, she said hello to whoever was in the girl's room, went into a stall and retched until she vomited. Then, she'd take out a carefully wrapped toothbrush, brush her teeth, shape her hair, touch up the mascara and hang out with preppies like Joey Ebersol until the bell rang.

Claire skipped school sometimes to jam with Noah. He played sax under the eucalyptus tree and she stood next to him fooling around on her clarinet. Then they'd switch. And as the music lifted, the liquid notes made hot, wild skywriting. Music was their reason for breathing and in that welder's light of late afternoon, jamming wistful and sweet, she could swear that the clouds and the blueness moved with their wind.

"That was good," Claire said, resting, knees up, her back leaning against the tree.

He hadn't been avoiding her, but they were both embarrassed. It was intense and scary. Things had moved too fast so they stuck to music, their common language.

Noah took autotech and offered to check Virginia's carburetor. She had been having some trouble. Claire said, "I'm surprised her crapola car still runs."

Noah said, "I forgot to tell you. Some guys at my school keyed this new girl's beemer. She's so loaded. She doesn't even pay for the gas." Noah went to Sunrise, a school of rejects as he called it. This new girl came from South Africa where they danced in clubs. "And get this, they have these raves where like 400 people come and every drug you can think of is laid out on the table. Like a buffet."

Claire and Noah would come in for a soda pop, and Claire noticed strangers started to call. Someone left a message on the answering machine: "I'm responding to your ad. I have two kids of my own and would love to talk to you. I make the boys dinner at about 6:15. Call me then at…" It was a librarian's voice, female.

Then another: "I am not afraid of AIDS. My brother died of it. I'm a marketing V.P. at a biotech company in town and I'd like to help you." This voice was clipped like a show dog's, but the fur was made of compassion. Another female voice.

A few days later: "Virginia, this is Katey. I'm a lawyer, a feminist and a mother. Not in that order. Your ad was powerful—a reflection of a woman of valor. I'd love to meet you for an interview."

Claire wondered. Was she also turning gay on me? That or she was trying to hire some crusader or advocate. Or was she going to create a project or foundation, or was she going to be interviewed on TV?

Claire moved her bookbag to the bedroom and called Talia, her best friend, who was just like Claire except she had boobs, a D average and a mother who still wore ruffled aprons if you could believe it. They talked for an hour about Talia's great love, Nathan, and the girl trying to steal him away and how far Talia'd go with him. "Maybe after six months, I would do it," she said. "I'm not sure."

"Yeah."

Then, Claire told her, half-reluctantly, half-relieved.

Talia was confused. Incredulous. "You bought the pregnancy test way before you even did it?"

"Yeah," Claire said.

"Why didn't you tell me before?"

"I don't know."

"Did you ever think of buying a rubber first?" Talia asked.

"I didn't want one."

"Geez," Talia added, "That's not what they mean by being prepared."

"I know. I guess I have my own ideas about family planning," Claire kidded.

Talia asked, "OK. So, did you take the test yet?"

"I'm afraid to."

"Yeah, being prego would suck big-time."

"What if I'm not pregnant? If all I have to show for it is nothing," Claire said.

"Then you celebrate!"

"Celebrate nothing?"

"Claire, you're crazed. So…was it good? I mean, I'm holding out and all, you're not going to influence me, but was it really something?"

Claire stared at Georgia O'Keeffe's cow skull (her dad had bought the print and framed it for her).

"It was OK."

"That's it? Just OK."

"Yeah."

"Does it hurt?"

"Yeah."

"Wow."

Then Talia figured out which creative lie to tell her mother because they just *had* to stay out after their curfew Saturday night to hear Nathan's band, Hazardous Waste, play downtown. Talia would say she's sleeping over Claire's; Claire would butter up her mama with sweets. "Who knows?" Claire said. "Nathan might even let me jam with them."

A few nights later Claire heard that dry cough and shortness of breath. It was like him again when he was here. She'd remind her mother in the morning to start taking her vitamin C again.

Talia dropped Claire off after school and said, "Bah-bye Claireygirl." Their front door was open. Claire could see her mama drinking wine on the patio with another lady. The house smelled like Lysol Country Scent.

Mama wheezed like an old lady. "Beggin yours. Oh, Claire, come here, come meet someone." Mama used her borrowed voice when strangers were present. She stood up so officially.

"Lydia, this is Claire. Isn't she beautiful? Claire, say hello to Lydia Murray."

Claire had on her grunge workshirt, baggy jeans and a new rash of zits on her forehead. But mothers were supposed to say their kids were beautiful for the sake of their self-esteem.

"Nice to meet you," Claire nodded. Lydia looked like an older version of Rochelle Miller, the girl in her class who got pregnant and had to leave school. Lydia's teeth were tiny and her mouth seemed quiet but she had on earrings with jade balls and silver hearts that seemed to do the talking for her anyway.

"Your mom showed me your picture," Lydia said demurely while her ears made music.

Mama sat down, but Lydia didn't. She looked like she needed to say more.

"My husband and I lost our little girl in a car accident."

"Bummer," Claire said to the stranger. Talia's neighbor's father had been hit by a car in Escondido. How did she know her mother? "How do you know my mother?"

"The ad in the paper."

Virginia reached for both wine glasses and the plate of American cheese on Ritz crackers, her hors d'oeuvres.

Claire didn't miss her father very much because fathers weren't much of a commodity in her neighborhood. They lived near apartments and little bungalows on the old side of Solana Beach behind the Carl's Junior near the Mexican migrant workers and skinny mothers with kids. There were groups of young Mexican guys, one old Chinese launderer nearby, but no fathers.

They had a sweet yellow stucco house with a flowerbox of half dead petunias out Mama's window and most of the women carried groceries home on foot and walked in their flip-flops to check the rusted mailboxes for the dreamed-of child support checks that usually didn't come. Some got welfare, some got drunk.

Mrs. Hernandez's daughter became a lawyer and told a few ladies outside Dairy Queen that 87% of California kids eligible for child support don't get a dime. Claire's mama said that was too depressing and she needed Drano and some fruit cocktail in the can. Ange McKay told LaShea's mother what else is new, and Pea Brain and Josie hot-rodded by in Josie's Camaro with plush red interior seats. He called it "El Fuego."

Claire's father had been away for years. Before she got into music, she played ball by herself. He drank, painted all night, left for L.A. for days. For awhile she tried to get him to teach her baseball, take her rollerblading at Mission Beach. She even dabbled in painting for awhile. They talked about the German Expressionists, lonely and isolated figures like Nolde and Munch, who painted her favorite painting, "The Scream," with its wavy lines of terror. She liked their distorted emotions and heightened reality. Too bad Dad couldn't leave that world for the boring stadium of catch. He and Mama would fight about Mama having to work so much and Claire figured fathers had showings. Then, like shadows, they disappeared.

Towards the end of May, days of unusual humidity were followed by relentless rain. A Korean lady in a raincoat stood on the patio with lots of grocery bags at her feet. Who were these women? Then one night, a towering, curly-haired, slim woman was in the kitchen. They got threatening calls about faggots and tainting the neighborhood and going to hell. Finally Claire asked her mother to start explaining.

"I've placed a personal ad," Virginia said like it was just a coupon, like it was no big deal. She picked Claire up from the community center pool twice a week in their ratty old slugbug. Sometimes Claire got a ride with Talia, who had her own car, or Noah. Their big swim meet was the next day so one night Claire stayed extra long. She was starving, it was dark and chilly and her mother's car was overheated. Claire got in, slammed the door and Virginia signaled left. She asked her mama about the personal ad. Mama said, "They call it personal for a reason." Claire had a ton of homework and couldn't be bothered. They were the only car for miles.

Her mother had the rash again on her arms and face that they attributed to the no-name detergent. Virginia told Claire she was going to the doctor, but she didn't tell Claire until later that they inserted a long tube into her lungs for a visual exam and biopsy. She didn't tell her daughter she had the beginnings of PCP, a form of pneumonia. Claire was sitting cross-legged in a beanbag chair at Robbie's listening to Nirvana.

Robbie told Claire the whole neighborhood was abuzz. "Your mother has advertised in the personals, looking for a mother for you."

Claire's heart beat like a pathetic bird.

"She requires resumes, references…She even sets up interviews like it was a real job."

When Claire tore home, Mama was in the bath for a soak. This was highly irregular. Usually the bathtub was too dirty and Mama too busy. She had gone all out with a white jasmine candle launching little smoke spiffs and a sweet scent, even Eric Clapton background music.

"Mama, we need to talk. Now." The door wasn't even shut. *Layla, you got me on my knees. Layla.* Mama left most drawers open and doors ajar—their knobs still warm—as she was always in the process of doing something or going somewhere.

"I almost named you Layla. Your daddy liked that name too. OK, sweetness." She coughed again. Her eyes were feverish and Claire knew she was getting run down. She moved the plastic shower curtain amassed with little daisies back and her breasts bobbed in the gray water.

On the sink were Claire's dad's Bactrim and Pentamidine next to some little green soaps. On the toilet top sat the razor her dad used and Virginia borrowed for her legs, and a wilting fern in a basket. Claire leaned against the sink.

"I don't want another mother."

"Baby, I have no kin who'll take you in." Virginia put her Salem out. "My sister, Wanda, is worthless. It's started. We both know what's gonna happen. The fevers, the infection in my lung, that constant cough. Then you're going to do the things you never should have like go to the Bahamas." There was that wild twist again, an amazing wrap-around skirt that Claire could never get the hang of. *Mama* always wanted to go to the Bahamas, not her.

"No. You can't," Claire said.

"Claire."

"Nooo," Claire screamed. "Noooo," she cried. "You can't leave me too. Not you. Please don't leave me."

Mama's eyes flew open like a wide awake doll's and she bolted out of the bath and hugged Claire tight and rocked her too forcefully.

Who would want Claire in the mornings when her breath is bad? Who'll help her if she gets food poisoning again at the Sea Harbor Grill and throws up in the car? And oh God, who'll call her Pretty Baby while she pops a pimple?

"Mama. Daddy gave up; you're stronger."

The wetness came through Claire's clothes. She slipped Claire into the warm water fully dressed, dropping some drops of vanilla oil in. And then she got in and her arms felt velvety and they were both in the bathtub like it was an everyday thing.

"I've got to go to Mexico like Daddy did and buy the Ribavirin and isoprinosine." Virginia usually couldn't even pronounce "encyclopedia" but they had so much experience with these drugs.

Claire knew she gave her heart away that night to her mother, Virginia Graham. And she never expected to get it back again. Real love must be like water in your ears muffling all the notes and murmurings, like drains clogging, like holding your sorrow in so tight that no bubbles escape. Everything is held down. Nothing is ransomed in real love.

Real love must be the tightest sucking in of breath, a hold so pure and blue, the deepest blue you can imagine.

And then you let go and peace or morning comes like Virginia talking then so calm about Mexico. No other mother will have her shape; the others will be diminishers of dreams. Virginia said she'd take the red trolley downtown and then the shuttle into Tijuana and Claire should just go to Robbie's or Talia's if she weren't back by six.

But it was too late.

Every day after today, Claire thought, I will sabotage the kindnesses of strangers. Every night after tonight I will read those silly Louise Hay healing books to my mother while she sleeps. I'll buy crystals, consult horoscopes, get positive. I'll demand information from those doctors at Scripps Hospital, I'll become religious. Somehow, if I force all my energies into a faith…

It is up to me to find a way to keep my mother.

Act II

(June & July)

White Nightgowns (Renata)

♦

Renata pointed out to Molly the spires of the castle-like Mormon Church. They took in the wide expanse of La Jolla, a breathtaking view, beyond the pool. "The garden was designed by the most expensive landscape designer in Rancho Santa Fe," Renata announced. Then Renata said she swam every night; her calf and thigh muscles were getting stronger. Renata picked off wilted petals from her carefully landscaped patio as she and Molly walked back into the Meyers' living room.

Molly said, "I saw your house in the May issue of *San Diego Home and Garden*."

Renata looked around her own home at the Oriental rug, leather couch, Mondrian print, contemporary sculptures, glass table. "The magazine called it a 'thoroughly modern home,' didn't they?" she asked rhetorically. Michael insisted on quality. They lived about $200,000 above their means.

Molly sat a little formally on the couch. "It's beautiful."

Renata said, "It's cold and pretentious. I collect photography, Kertesz and Bresson, beautiful black-and-white prints, and antiques. I love antiques-" Molly canvassed the room, looking for the antiques. "They're not out. Michael says this isn't a mildewed European chateau. I guess we all have to live in the here-and-now. It's funny, you and I. You're trying to run away from history and I'm looking for it."

Renata was tired of being a prop in a perfect house, tired of being on the outside of things. Not baking Bliss cookies was one small thing. She and Michael had definitely drifted. She looked at Molly. Molly reminded her of a pioneering Oregon woman, someone in a Willa Cather story or a story about hunters or Irish myths. She had strong hands, poetic eyes.

"He's very handsome, your husband." Molly was uncomfortable and her voice tapered off.

Renata put her wine glass on the coaster and leaned forward as if to whisper a secret. "I miss the trees. The white oaks and elms and snow days by the fireplace. Real things, real people, not this artificial sunniness."

Molly said, "You'd love Washington. But did you see the Torrey Pines here? I have the most beautiful ride driving to Scripps and home. They're so rare, too. I read that back east some of the elms have that fungus spread by bark-beetles. Oh, that's depressing." Molly brushed imaginary crumbs off the table.

Renata was jubilant. Nothing wrong with blight, little creatures. "I had an ant farm when I was a kid. William just had an earthworm for a pet a few months ago when it rained. Claire Graham baby-sat and they did experiments on mealworms."

"Claire is a wonderful girl."

"Everything here is a sunny pool. All the women with their Wonder bras, all this positive thinking crap. Claire said mealworms eat oatmeal and apple. Sounds like my breakfast. She is a special girl, isn't she?"

Renata thought of their innocence, that kiss at the pool. "Listen to the crickets," Renata stopped. "I miss the owls swooping down. An owl can hear a mouse move under inches of snow."

"You are a walking encyclopedia," Molly softly responded.

"Yeah, I somehow retain ridiculous facts. And Arden—are things going well?"

"Yes, too good to be true."

Renata had already gone back to the pale silver bark of beech trees in winter and how a few ghostly leaves rustled back east. You could see your breath like smoke as you tramped a path to school and the salt-truck sprinkled white on the road which appeared to have only new snow but was ice-packed underneath. The sky was steel. The bus would be delayed by the weather conditions. Her mother was home frying eggs, the blue number from Dachau peeking out from her sleeve. Her father would be lathering his face, attending to the ministrations of the shave, before laying a crisp napkin on his lap, eating Mother's breakfast and reading the morning paper. Then off to the bank until the evening when he and Mother would discuss politics, her father showering Renata with adoring looks, her mother guarding a reliquary of dreams, saying, "You might as well apply to the best law schools you can, Renata" and the diamante flakes falling in the darkness outside the kitchen window curtained in guipure lace.

Molly admired the Chagall print of the milkmaid and the cow and the happy Russian village which hung over the fireplace, behind the braided black candlesticks. Renata stood up, moved to touch the picture's edge, "This was my grandfather's. My grandfather on my father's side was from Russia. He was quite a man. He was a wealthy businessman in Brooklyn, very established, with a trimmed beard. He found out he had lung cancer—he smoked two packs of Lucky Strikes a day—and from the day he learned his diagnosis, he scheduled "conferences" as he called them. With associates, with family members. In these conferences, he confessed to each person whatever grudges he held against them. Can you imagine? He insulted us, told us what he didn't like. Everyone stumbled out of his library exhausted and drawn."

They laughed.

"Truth isn't always a good thing. Then again," Molly said, standing so she too could caress the frame of the art, "people hear whatever they want to hear."

"That's true." Renata pinched the two wine glasses together and took them to the kitchen.

"I mean you can reveal something true, but that doesn't necessarily mean you are honest." Molly raised her voice so the absent Renata could hear. "You can tell just one part of the story. You're an attorney. You know better than I do about shades of the truth and holding back."

Renata reentered the room. "Here is a copy of the restraining order that was filed. He has to stay 100 yards from your home. I'm sure you have nothing to worry about. Let's get together again. This was nice."

"Thanks, Renata. He's stayed away so long, I wonder. Anyway, thank you for helping me with the restraining order. And for Arden—he's so wonderful."

"You remind me of something. I don't know when I lost it." They hugged uncomfortably, barely. Molly's scent was like that of the woods on the first day of spring.

The whole family—Renata, Michael, Jane and William—sat in lounges by the JCC pool on a mostly gloomy June day while their own pool was being cleaned. Renata imagined the ocean waves crawling toward her, remembered swimming in the wind-protected La Jolla Cove with Michael, the way this handsome guy from Laguna Beach, USC-grad, had beguiled her with his athletic style and strength. His strong thigh muscles propelled him, and like a speedboat hydroplaning, he thrust through the water. She loved that arc of his back and his conceit. She had never seen the butterfly stroke done so effortlessly. He had ended up a partner at Gray Stein Fredericks, the biggest corporate law firm in town, through family connections.

Now she realized salt water gave more buoyancy than a pool's. Not only that—he had taken the butterfly stroke and mastered it, but it was the only stroke he did well. *She had been a swim champion.* Not just individual medley events, but the 4 X 100m relay medley—all four strokes, plus turns, starts, and finishes. She had trophies lining the shelves of her room back in her parents' house. He swam in the cool part, in the shadow, and part of her from then on felt brighter than him.

Michael tickled Jane, who squealed with laughter as he threw her in the water.

Michael sat on the chair next to her, grabbed the sunscreen and reminded her, "So we're getting some bucks back this year. Maybe we can take off for a weekend this summer and go to Baja or up the coast to Big Sur again. Huh, honey? Doesn't that sound good? We need a break, you and me."

"Maybe. That sounds fine," she said. There was no anger left, only a clarity. The marriage was over. Things just worked out certain ways. If she had to admit it, she felt clear-headed pain, like sharp pangs on a sunny day. She watched the dark hairs flatten on Michael's greased leg.

"Mommy, Willie's gonna eat me for wunch," Jane tattled as she climbed out of the pool. They had been in for almost an hour.

"Comere," Renata said, putting her Ray-Bans on top of her head and scooting forward. "Take a rest. Let me see if you have those lines on your fingers. Give me your fingers."

Renata asked Michael to move out a few minutes before Virginia dropped off Claire to baby-sit. As Virginia waved and drove her VW away, Claire yelled from the doorway, "Take your vitamins, Mama." Michael stood in the living room, his shirt crumpled, "I'm not leaving my kids. We're a family. I care about those kids."

Renata stood her ground on the first stair. "I can't live a lie anymore. I've become a lie, Michael."

Michael said, "Honey…"

Renata said, "The kids will adjust."

"But I'll miss them so much," Michael's voice cracked.

Claire absorbed the tension, looked at both of them and said maybe she'd go check on the kids. She passed Renata as she mounted the stairs. Claire's tee shirt said, "Music rules."

Michael moved out four days after Renata was awarded a promotion, on the first day of camp for the kids, and a day after Carmella went on vacation to Mexico.

The second night after he was gone, after their favorite lasagna dinner and raspberry dessert and a bubble bath, Renata presented the kids with a new goal. She told William and Jane they were going to work on twelve virtues—one for every month of the year. "Virtues are good traits or good things. It's a way to do good, take good actions. Like, let's see, kindness, trust, honesty, patience…those kinds of things are virtues."

William carried the full laundry basket from the dryer because he was a big 6-year old. "Why did Carmella have to go on vacation? I don't want to do this."

Renata said, "Hey—"

Jane had a special job: locating her socks in the pile and matching them in pairs. They all sat on the king-sized bed and decided which virtue to choose for July as they folded the clean clothes.

The phone rang. The kids froze like it was an alarm. "Hi Michael. Fine. OK.," she put the receiver to her shoulder and said, "Daddy wants to say night-night."

Jane looked at her feet and pouted. "I want Daddy to come back." William was all confidence. He told his father his tooth was loose and he learned how to do a flip off the diving board. Renata's tongue moved over her own teeth, remembering the texture of a loose tooth pushing back and forth, the yanking out of the tooth by its root, the hole that remained. Everybody has spaces in their smartness, places of feeling emptiness, places they don't understand.

For a minute or so after they hung up, nobody said a word. Renata waited for her children. Usually she fit them in her hand and directed them, lightly nudged, jerked them—ever so slightly—to make sure they were following her. But now she had to wait for their grief or anger or understanding. And she waited. For their pain or acceptance or blame as history took its course. Jane concentrated on matching socks. William folded the monogrammed mauve towel into perfect squares. She thought the quiet would burn a hole through her heart, but she waited anyway. Until she could wait no more.

"So, let's pick a virtue. All this month, what good thing should we do?" she asked, folding William's one jean leg on top of the other and then folding it again in half.

"You could buy me toys for kindness," exclaimed William.

Renata laughed and Jane asked, "Are you happy at us, Mommy?"

"Yes, honey."

William asked, "What's Daddy doing?"

Renata picked up the maroon, thin-striped pillowcase and couldn't answer. The kids helped her fold the white sheet next, meeting at the corners. "Giving and sharing is a nice idea. I know—why don't we start with forgiveness?"

"But I wasn't bad," William stated emphatically.

Renata shook out her white cotton nightgown one, two times. It made a noise like it was flapping in the wind. She looked at the delicate curved neckline. "Every day this month let's figure out a way to forgive."

She turned it around and held it to her body like she was sizing up a new dress. Her left hand held it to her chest, her other hand smoothed the belly area.

Haunted by white nightgowns.

She added it to the pile and picked up more laundry to fold.

William said, "Nah. Forgiveness is no good. I don't like that. Let's pick another idea, Mom."

A few hours later, after William and Jane were fast asleep, the doorbell rang. Renata opened the door. A police officer stood there, loosening his collar.

"I almost killed a fuckin kid today," he said in a thick New York accent, a tiny stump of a cigarette in his teeth. He leaned one hand against the house. "A little creep was spray-paintin the patrol car, if you can believe this. So I took one more bite of the donut, stuffed it in my mouth—the sugar kind I didn't want to get all over me, you know I keep myself neat—and he whirls around and thinks I don't know from nothin, but I do. So he's got the peanut from gang graduation cocked and I'm thinkin how the guys in Brooklyn are gonna go apeshit when they hear a jellyroll done me cause I'm dustin the sugar offa me. So's I quick whip out my piece and tell him to suck my dick. There we are both aimin at each other and he says, 'My ole man's dead. It's ashame, it's ashame. My mama says I got his artist ways.'"

Jake was silent. "Bidda bing, bidda bang. That was it; I couldn't get the dildo. I let go. Like that. I let him walk away. He was 11, tops."

"Come in, Jake. You want some coffee?"

"The kids asleep?"

"Yes. Sit down." She took out mugs and poured coffee.

As Jake sat he said, "Well, now you can stay home with the kids. Good. He's givin you money, right?"

"I don't want to stay home," Renata said.

"Michael was too Goyish anyway. At the wedding, we called him white bread. Don't get me wrong, my mother, your mother—they wouldn't say nothin bad about your choice, of course, Renata. You both were sharp kids, smart and all. All those years, we knew you'd come out on top, shining. Call the maid and let's go. I want you should listen to some music, get out."

"She's on vacation. Jakey, I can't go out now."

"You got any sugar?"

"No sugar."

"You could use some sweetenin." He poured milk and stirred his coffee. "You're so ramrod, so tightassed. Man. Ah right. Tomorrow night, we're goin out."

"What are you doing, Jake? I don't need company."

"Maybe company needs you, huh? Maybe the cartooner I almost evaporated is on my mind. Just because I'm a talkuh don't mean I'm an idiot…"

"Jakey, You know I care about you."

"See, when that kid said his daddy croaked, it all came back. Your parents and my mother, the marching, the nightmares of the camps. We grew up together, but I still don't know how you do it. Those stupid, old photographs. How do ya forget? "

Renata said, "I don't forget. I just put it aside, or replace it with something el—"

"They were just past bein teenagers…"

"Jake, you invited us to visit, then showed us around when we moved here. And coming by every month or two, taking the kids down to the station…"

"I told you ya'd love San Diego."

"But Jake, you're not responsible for me."

"The rabbi said last Friday—"

"You go regularly now?"

"I know our parents are through with God, but I need to make sense of things. There's gotta be some order out of chaos. I can't just eat a bagel and be a Jew.

It's not really about believing, it's more about taking action to clean up this fuckin hellhole we live in, make it a safer, better place. Hey, maybe all cops are honorary Jews. Boy, that would go over big with the boys at the precinct. So let me do my mitzvah here."

"I've been thinking a lot about forgiving and forgetting lately. OK, Jake. Tomorrow night, where are we going?"

"That's a big surprise."

The lights dimmed. A woman tapped her heel softly, then again. Louder. The spotlight came on and her metallic skirt swirled. Stamp, click, faster and faster. Her head flung back proudly, orange flowers in her hair, as she stomped the beat and her ankle bracelets shimmied. She swerved and undulated, her arms like snakes. Faster and faster, her black hair sweeping the air, she pounded the floorboards. A vibrant dance flaming, shaking and shimmering and twirling. "Ole." The crowd applauded wildly.

"I've never seen the Flamenco," Renata said breathless.

Jake ordered another drink for them both.

When they left Cafe Sevilla, Fourth Avenue was teeming with couples on this Saturday night.

"I remember when the Gaslamp Quarter was a good place to get your butt tattooed and to meet a ladyfriend on one of those second-floor walkups. So, you good?"

"That was wonderful. Let's stop somewhere. I don't want to leave yet."

"Let's go dancin."

"I don't dance," Renata stated.

"That's your problem."

"Jake," Renata said.

They entered a cafe. "Hey, I'm not a lawyer or doctor or nothin. We might've ended up in different places, but we have the same roots." Jake put his arm around her to direct her to the table.

Renata was emphatic: "We ended up in the same place." She sat down and Jake pushed her chair in.

Jake smiled broadly. "You liked them tapas, Renata, that we had before?"

They ordered coffee and dessert.

"I don't get it, Jake. How does religion fit into all this?"

"I give back the R.M.P., hightail out of the goddam precinct, change my clothes, no tin, and go to temple on Friday nights. For about six months now. That's it. No fuckin big deal."

"And tonight?"

"It's Saturday night. Shabbat is over and it's time to fuckin party."

"Your mouth is a sewer," she offered amiably.

"There's no holy and profane, sweetheart. Buber said there's just the holy and the not-yet-holy. Excuse me," and he called the waitress. "Sweetheart, I don't want none of those Kahlua or cool-whip drinks. Just pour some Bacardi in this coffee. Straight. Thank you."

Renata couldn't take her eyes off him. "I don't know about religion. Spirituality is OK."

"I'm not lookin for a way to explain this world. I'm just tryin to bring God into it."

"How do you do that?" she asked.

"You make ordinary stuff kind of special or Godly. I say thanks for letting me wake up. Hello up there. Thanks for coffee, this sunny day. Thanks for giving me strength and by the way, I'm gonna need some more later. I'm not there yet. But I've always been a little slow."

"Is this about Dachau?" Renata asked.

"It's about goodness and giving, your life having value…"

"But—"

"…ultimate justice."

"But there isn't any."

"Then why are you a lawyer and me a cop?"

Renata shrugged, I don't know.

"It wasn't that his old man was taken out, that both-of-us-was-fatherless bullshit. You see, it was just I could hear my mother sayin I had my daddy's ways…"

"Then Ma married Bill, a hell of a nice conner. He sells dental supplies now. Did I tell ya he sells this dental articulatin paper to dentists in Brooklyn and then he resells them the same paper they just bought. What a racket."

"How's your brother, Joey?" Renata asked.

"Joey's Joey," Jake said. "I saw your folks at Hanukkah when I was back there. You don't call much, they said."

Jake took her hands in his and kissed her knuckles. "The way I look at it, Renata, everything I do is in spite of motherfuckin doubt. In spite of suckin evil. In spite of this million mile wall of shit. I keep findin good. It kind of hits me in the face when I'm not lookin and more often lately."

"We have a long history, don't we?" Renata said.

"Are you talkin about the Jewish thing? Or are you talkin about you and me?" he flirted.

The Pool (Dorie)

◆

When Dorie wasn't pouring liquor in her hair, she was speaking out. The bagger packed the groceries too heavy. That guy in front of her on Pearl Street should have moved his ass. Maybe she was especially angry because she hadn't done the wild thing in what seemed like years now and all that excitement was pent up in her. Plus, she was working all the time. Where was time for her? Time for fun?

Hmmm. An ice cold rinse off on a steamy June morning. She smoothed luxurious peppermint body lotion on her cone-shaped breasts. Ahhh.

Outside the peeling white house, Dorie and Paul were at it again.

"I need a car. It's a used car. Christ. Give me a break, Dorie," Paul sighed with disgust. His pecs looked bigger like he had been going to the gym more. They were outside by the pink geraniums, arguing as usual on a hot, bright June day.

"I'm tired of hearing your money excuses," Dorie said. Dorie was now working days and *four* nights every other week at the Pannikin..

Paul tried to ignore her as he leaned against his just-waxed Nissan, his arms crossed defensively. "I'm doing my best. That's all I can say."

"Well, it's not good enough. Do you know how much it costs for camp for both of them, doctor bills, insurance, rent, everything? You're the father. Take responsibility, you bastard."

"Just get the girls, Dorie. I don't have to listen to this."

"Yes you do." Dorie was seething.

"Hey, did you see the movie, "Roots"? He looked her mini-dress up and down.

"Yeah."'

"Well, us guys are the slaves, and the bosses, Riley and Smith, are the slave drivers. OK? That's what trying to get work is like."

"Work at Burger King while you're waiting."

"I'm trying everything, Dorie. Get off my case and get the girls. I don't have to listen to this anymore."

"I don't like being put in the position of nagging and begging. You better get some money to me before the end of this week or else."

"Threatening me isn't going to get you the money any faster."

"I'll see your sorry ass in court."

As he and the kids drove away, Dorie couldn't believe she was standing there alone. They would listen to old blues by Crystal Pier in Pacific Beach or take their bikes on the ferry to Coronado and ride all day. She married him soon after they met her freshman year at San Diego State. They had this crazy ceremony on the rollercoaster at Belmont Park, which he went along with for her. Paul had a killer smile. He used to call her "Dorie, the force of nature."

Relatives criticized and her Mom wasn't thrilled, but even though she was only 19, she was a quick "Lerner" as her literature professor teased after she took his name. She already knew she wanted a straight arrow guy, some cute kids, merry times. She also wanted to be a crack reporter. Maybe for a midsize paper here or in the southwest. That's why ever since who-knows-when she ate fish to get a bigger brain. She cut out the red meat, the fat of gossip and got lean and strong on news that counts.

At daycare the next morning, Natalie refused her yogurt. She wouldn't eat her breakfast again. Four days now. "Why aren't you eating, sweetie?" She wouldn't answer. "Tell me please." Dorie couldn't stand it.

"If I eat my bweakfast you will weave for work."

"Oh," Dorie said. "Nat-"

I always thought I'd be a real mother—not one for 45 minutes in the morning and two hours at night. She hugged her little girl and fought back the tears.

At the end of the day, she slipped out of her heels, wiggled out of her skirt and sank into a chair at the kitchen table in blouse and stockings. Natalie was irritable. That evening the bumps were everywhere. Chickenpox. Shit. Dorie's mother worked in Fashion Valley…Who'd take care of her? Will a baby-sitter put calamine lotion on her sores or even baby-sit if she's contagious? Claire's in school. Dorie had no more sick or vacation days left at the office and she needed the tips from The Pannikin at night. Shit, shit.

She frantically called around. Her boss at the real estate office asked, "Can't you just get a baby-sitter from the phone book?" Her mother took off one day and kept the girls overnight so Dorie could work at the office, then waitress. She took off with no pay Thursday and Friday. Carrying a sick child around was like carrying a laundry bag filled with wet clothes. Claire saved her ass and baby-sat Friday night for free while Dorie waitressed, and Ian spelled her over the weekend. How was she going to pay the bills this month without those days at Coldwell Banker and the nights at Pannikin?

Natalie recovered and things improved. Renata suggested they take a break and go fishing. Dorie's dad loved the idea, and he took Dorie and the girls fishing off a pier in Shelter Island. He bought the girls these cute kiddy rods at Target and his white hair ruffled in the breeze as he bent down and patiently explained to the girls, "If we catch baby fish, we throw them back because they're too little. OK?" Livie understood immediately: "OK. We just kill the parents."

Dorie couldn't afford to take her lovelies to Sea World or the Zoo, but on weekends they went on long walks at Torrey Pines Reserve, had picnics with salami sandwiches, honeydew and plums in the park, built sandcastles at La Jolla Shores. She found cute stuff at the gently-used shops. But there was no getting around the medical insurance and daycare costs. The JCC gave her a scholarship for camp and let her pay for daycare in installments, sometimes late. But her paychecks at both jobs barely covered her car insurance, rent and food as it was.

She passed a homeless family living out of their Pinto. At least they didn't have to sleep in the car tonight, she thought. It's getting close though. Dorie made the girls stay in the car for hours so she could feel what it would be like. Livie said she was hot and kept rolling the window up and down. "Mom, let's go," she demanded. Dorie said a few more minutes. How were they going to manage? Dorie drove to her parents' house. Her dad walked over to the car and said, "I'm not letting you down, Dorie. You'll do fine; you just need a hand."

He gave his hand all right: big, strong, some hair on the knuckles and it passed a white envelope through the open car window. Again and again. Until he suggested she get a lawyer because Paul was too many child support payments behind and this was getting serious. That's when she hired Renata.

It was a boring work day. Tom's house fell out of escrow, Lena had some looky-loos, Sheryl blabbed on and on about the Jenny Craig diet. Dorie thought as she filed some papers, "I give my girls the worst of myself. I save the best of myself for work and strangers."

She scooted over to the ATM machine to get some money. She was afraid to see the balance. After the divorce papers were served, she changed her pin number to "free." The screen revealed that she had $11 in checking and her savings account had been closed due to lack of sufficient funds. Being free was expensive.

By the time she pulled into the JCC parking lot to get the girls she was choking down the tears. As self esteem goes down, thoughts of men go up her girlfriend Lexxie had joked. Dorie just had to be with someone tonight. Summer was here and this was getting too awful.

Jason Dare played in one of the local bands in P.B. and was very hot-looking. He had long lashes, piercing brown eyes, full lips, a great butt and long blond hair. But once the girls went to sleep and he got under the covers with Dorie, it was about as exciting as a Waltons rerun. Come to think of it, MTV would have juiced her more. Talk about a big yawn of a sex machine.

She made him leave when the sun rose. A bit later, Livie rubbed her eyes and came padding in to watch cartoons and Natalie came over to hug Dorie and breathe her wombat breath as she snuggled into Dorie's lap. Dorie suddenly understood why her mother lifted her eyes from the paper and her Maxwell House coffee, the buttery light through the kitchen window, when Ian and she woke up. She finally got it.

The news around the pool was that Renata and her husband separated. It's a shame, but at least she's well off; she's got a house, a good job. Man, maybe she could hook some wild orthodontist!

Renata didn't mention the separation. She said that she and Virginia Graham met at the pool Mondays and Wednesdays. Molly Wright was sometimes there too. Dorie's dad paid for the girls' swimming lessons on Wednesdays anyway. Why not meet them? Dorie said yeah, OK.

On Wednesday, the JCC lockerroom smelled dank, like used Reeboks, boiled eggs and steamy rose deodorizer. Claire sat on a bench, dazed. She had dark hair, not as dark as her mother Virginia's, and a softer mouth. She was holding her bathing suit in her lap. "Noah and I broke up."

"Why? You guys look so cute together." Dorie sat on the bench next to her.

Claire said, "Noah doesn't want me, really want me." Olivia and Natalie sang Ring around the Rosie, moving in a circle, while women getting out of the shower and putting their sneakers on darted around them.

"Is there another girl?"

"He dumped me, Dorie. He thinks *I'm* using *him*," she laughed.

"You're using him for his bod?"

Claire got serious fast. "I've got nothing." The girls sang "All fall down" and fell to the floor giggling.

Dorie put her arm around Claire. Claire said, "Mama is trying to hire a mother for me. You can't just hire a new mother. That's so ridiculous."

The girls started the song again. Claire said flatly, "Everybody leaves me."

"Get your suit on, girl. It's too hot today and that pool is just calling us."

Claire said, "I'm sick of hanging out with my mother and her friends and hearing about their problems."

"I'm your friend, too, you know. And luckily I have no problems. C'mon."

From across the pool, Dorie saw Noah walk. He walked by Claire. Claire looked at him and then away before his eyes had a chance to catch hers. Claire cuddled the redhead's new baby, kissing its forehead so tenderly. Then she cradled it, smiling. She reluctantly gave the bundle back to the mother and sat down in a lounge.

"You OK now?" Dorie asked Claire, approaching the group in their usual spot by the shallow end and the snack bar. Dorie was running on nervous energy.

"Yeah. Welcome to the Single Mother's Club," joked Claire from the lounge as she rubbed Aveda sunscreen on her calf. She had on a cute salmon-colored textured bikini. The JCC pool was crowded in the late afternoon.

"Oh please," said Virginia, rearranging her royal blue one-piece with foam cups. "All mothers are single mothers. Right now I feel more like a roasted duck. Hello pretty girls." Virginia's lipstick looked phosphorescent orange like a moon rock.

"We have our tubes," boasted Natalie of the colorful lifesavers around her and her sister. "Hi Claire. Hi Mrs. Gwayam."

"Why," said Virginia, "they look like hula-hoops now, don't they?"

"Hi." Molly greeted Dorie and motioned to sit next to her. She delicately patted the seat. She was always soft-spoken. Her auburn hair cut modestly short, green eyes not too green and a Land's End suit just right. She was the only one in a chair, not in a lounge, sitting lady-like wearing a straw hat, quietly turning the pages of a book.

The girls splashed around in the shallow end by the steps and Dorie sat next to Molly. Livie blurted, "Here's a noogie-butt cannon bomb. Look, Mom." Dorie didn't.

Renata had just swum a few laps and walked gracefully from ten yards away, her gold locket shining, squeezing her hair into a ponytail. She wore a simple black suit, her fingernails and toenails painted the same rosy glaze.

"Dorie, hi. Why don't I pick up Natalie tomorrow and take her to my house to play with Jane?" Renata dabbed her towel to her face and Dorie noticed her pearl earrings were the exact color of her teeth.

"Natalie will be totally psyched," Dorie said. Renata followed Virginia and Claire to the snack bar.

"How's your daughter in college in Santa Barbara?" Dorie asked Molly, who was reading. Dorie stripped off her purple vinyl mini-dress. "Didn't you and Arden visit her?"

Molly looked up. Her voice was warm like polished walnut. "Yes, she's fine. It's strange, Dorie. Ocean Aquatics already met and there's Claire without Noah. I don't know what's going on between those two. Do you?" Dorie lied and said no. Molly continued, "Claire has a job for the summer at a record store and she's working a lot, but has she dropped him?"

"I know her old mama, Virginia, adores your son," Dorie said. Dorie wore her hot suit, the one with the zipper down the front, cut way high on the legs in acid green. The zipper was fluorescent pink.

Molly pretended like she wasn't blinded. "Virginia is already planning their honeymoon in Maui." She looked up as Virginia and Claire returned and addressed Virginia, "Aren't you?"

Virginia carried two Diet Cokes and a frozen yogurt. Claire grabbed the tab off her soda. "Mama, just let me know when my flight to Maui leaves, won't you?" Dorie was busy lotioning up; the coconut smell brought back every summer.

"Be careful, Natalie," Renata yelled jumping to her feet. She turned and scolded Dorie. "Are your girls okay over there?"

Damn. The girls were near the deep end. "Olivia, watch your sister. Watch Natalie!" Dorie yelled, exasperated. "Come closer to me. Both of you."

Livie said, "I have to do the noogie-butt pencil and the noogie-butt flip!"

Virginia slurped the soda through her straw. "Did you squeeze any water from the stone?"

"What?" Dorie asked.

"Has he paid up yet?" Virginia asked, referring to Paul.

"No, we're going to court next month."

"Well, California is advanced," Virginia stated.

Renata leaned forward and said to Virginia, "You think California is progressive? It ranks 47th nationally in collection of court-ordered child support. *Court ordered* support. But, Dorie, we'll do OK."

Great. Just great. "I'll get no money plus he doesn't even want the kids, but he's seeking custody," Dorie said, smearing sunscreen on her leg in jerky movements. She was always rushing…

"As soon as you ask to modify support now, the guys ask to modify custody. If they get the kids more, they pay less. It's an equation." Renata said coolly.

"Kids have it bad today. It makes me sick as a dog to think about them neglected kids." Virginia scooped a big glob of yogurt into her mouth. She wiped her lips with the napkin and smeared the orange lipstick. It reminded Dorie of a popsicle cream bar. But then for a moment, looking at Virginia's black hair and strong features, Dorie figured she might've once had Elizabeth Taylor's seductive intensity.

"Is it government or the dads to blame?" Dorie asked. She flipped through *Elle*, the magazine Virginia bought for Claire regularly, which Claire said was garbage and passed on to Dorie. Oh good. Dorie hadn't seen this issue. Politics and fashion were her passions.

Molly appeared quite serious. "Men are the government and the dads both. They don't get it because they don't raise the kids. You know, I think animal rights groups have more legislative power than children's rights groups. When Sam hurled Mr. T against the garage door, the animal rights protection agency followed up immediately. Child welfare's line was always busy."

"Hmmm," nodded Renata.

Molly swung her legs out, back again and stood up. "Let's just talk about men or clothes or our careers—" She took off her hat and shook her hair free.

"Career? Make that job. I don't want no epitaph saying 'Virginia Graham, Beloved Quality Control Supervisor', May she rest in peace."

"Can you imagine if motherhood was considered a career? If it was worth big bucks?" Molly said.

Claire said, "Then you'd all be rich!"

Dorie said, "My mother's such a good mother. No guy can come close. That's what I blame her for. She really screwed me up."

Virginia closed her eyes to the sun. Dorie happened to look at Claire and she was glued to every word.

Renata put her black Ray-Bans on and sank back into her lounge.

Dorie knew it was too perverted for words, but she saw that guy again. The great tan one who looked like a grad student. Gabe and she teased each other last time at the pool and he tried to dunk her. This time they started fooling around in the water. Most of the lifeguards had gone as it was after 5 PM, and not too many children remained. The cafe had closed. Well, he was an amazing kisser and then he was touching her and getting hard. They moved into a corner and she could feel his pull-buoy rub against her inner thigh. Quickly, he came inside her and they were doing it. Right there in the JCC pool close to dinnertime.

She couldn't stop. It was like she had been so hot and bothered for so long with no release. Unable to feel anything that filled her up. And she'd rather die than feel parched and empty. Here came this god, a water fantasy plugging the hole. She deserved this.

When she climbed out of the pool, Renata was holding a sobbing Natalie. "Natalie waded into the deep end. You might lose these girls, Dorie." She left abruptly.

Dorie took Natalie and said, "You okay?" She held her and tried to console her.

Virginia, Claire and little Livie were feasting on frozen strawberry fruitbars. Molly sat impassively, ignoring Dorie, a Jane Austen book face down on her lap.

"A few men watched. Some even began smokin," Virginia laughed. "Heck, hon, didn't you know we was all watchin you?"

"I was lost in my own world," Dorie said, flushed. She felt more relaxed afterwards than she had been since she and Paul were together. But she wasn't a pervert.

Virginia said, "I reckoned you just wanted to be reckless and give us a real smutty show while you were at it."

"Molly? Are you mad at me?"

Molly looked at the pool. She wouldn't look at Dorie. Only at the pool. "I lost myself too. First in a man, then my kids. I went under too."

"I can't explain it. Renata was pissed, huh? She seemed...Whoa." Dorie said.

"Well you left Livie and Natalie in the pool by their lonesome..." Virginia chided.

"It was dangerous," Molly added, returning to her book, but you could tell she wasn't reading.

Dorie hugged Natalie and Livie to her. Claire seemed embarrassed and looked at her feet.

Molly moved close to Dorie; her eyes bore into her. "You can't separate the woman part from the mother part."

"I was looking for the woman part?" Dorie asked.

That night, Virginia told Dorie she tossed; Renata said she stared at the ceiling until three; Molly gave Arden a book on Thomas Merton and they fell asleep during the news. Dorie didn't know how Claire managed. But Dorie slept like a baby.

Reaching and Extension Assists (Molly)

♦

Full moon in July. When it's a full moon, she felt it. She looked up from the bowl of flour and saw it beaming through her blue-and-white gingham curtains. All women have a tidal pull, but especially those of us born into summer, she thought. The moon tugged at her heart. Like a shredded sponge, pieces crumbled. Last month she and Arden kissed on a park bench. That full moon drew them like hungry nocturnal animals slipping on the rocks, pulled by an undercurrent.

She went and slipped. She let herself open to him and she swore how many times? She knew if she made love with him, she'd lose herself.

Today Renata gave her a print from the Picasso show in L.A. called "Weeping Women." It's exquisite. Renata wanted to join the Masters Swim program and though they're both reserved, Molly knew they respected one another. When Molly heard Renata and her husband separated, she wondered how much Virginia, Dorie and she had influenced her decision. Molly asked, "Will you have problems with your family about this?" Molly was thinking she was Catholic too. But Renata answered she was Jewish. One thing you can say for the Jewish people, they are survivors.

Renata sensed Molly's hesitancy in the pool (Renata seemed to feel with her body). Renata smiled graciously at Molly's progress. Renata was sleek as a thoroughbred. She swam like a natural. Molly wished she had her grace.

In May and June, Molly finally went in up to her knees. And then she could almost sit in the water. Still afraid to close her eyes, she didn't know if she'd ever submerge her head underwater, let alone her neck. Dorie, in her lycra and lace, didn't get how someone can't just dive right in. But Molly felt if she wrote a poem about drowning, Dorie would get it because she and Dorie had this affinity for words.

Molly was the timer yesterday for the 50-yard freestyle. She was proud that her son, Noah, swam it in one breath. His time was 35:12, Claire came in at 36:21. Noah told Molly he and Claire broke up. But he still liked the way Claire looked after her mother, and he wanted Molly to know he was looking after her too.

He joined the Police Athletic League the year before, and today his friend stopped by. Allowed in Noah's room, plastered with posters of basketball stars and messy as it was, Molly felt quite honored. But within a few minutes, his other friend Dave appeared and the three of them were talking about the recent World Cup soccer match. Dave had gone to USD where Sweden practiced and met some Germans who were traveling all over the U.S. to watch the Germans play. Dave couldn't believe that devotion. His other friend Ty had gone to Pasadena for the Brazil and Honduras Exhibition match and he said the chanting, seeing all the flags, how much the fans got into it and stuff was awesome. Time for Molly to leave.

Night…Typical June gloom days held over into July, but the nights had been clear. No word from Arden since yesterday's lunch. For over two months now, they had been accompanying each other. He had plans last night and tonight which she didn't ask him about, but maybe that's the way things were always going to be. Distrust seeped in over the years with Sam as easily as the blackness spread between the constellations. While the night-sky shook the stars down, Molly sat on her summer sheets and awaited the falling pieces.

It's like the fireworks from a week or two ago. Where did they land?

Fresh air might do me good, thought Molly. She told Noah and his friends to check on the soda bread in the oven; she was going out for a walk. Nights used to be something you could walk though, breathe in—leaves waxy and clean, dark green, the earth loam-rich. Take a trail through a forest, follow the trees. You could walk to free your thoughts; now you risk the rape of the night.

She felt Sam's sweaty, beefy fingers on her chin and neck…him forcing himself on her, slobbering on her neck…A man's right…But he'd always be sorry afterwards, they had two kids after all…He repented and she was supposed to forgive. Their vows were forever, he reminded her. He loved her, didn't she know that?

Growing up, she believed she could head toward a world of music and art and beauty (she grew up on a farm but she read a lot) by falling in love with the right man. Jeez Louise. It wasn't just the wrong man, it was the disfiguring romantic fantasy that love would open the right windows.

Now she opened her own windows, cleaned the screens and dreamed of the white picket fence every once in awhile. Maybe more lately—she admitted. But who has the perfect nuclear family anymore? Mariah is away, her first year at college, and probably relieved to be on her own. Molly surmised she was sleeping around, but wasn't sure.

Molly sometimes missed Seattle and Whidbey Island and Puget Sound and wet leaves in the rain. She worried about Mariah, who was much like Claire—independent, practical—but Mariah still believed bad things only happen if you let them happen. She didn't know about random fate, cruelty, the evil that flourishes even in good family gardens, the danger that is sometimes married to love. Molly stopped. What am I doing, a woman walking alone at night?

For weeks now, every night at midnight, someone calls and hangs up. An insect scratched at the walls of her stomach when she thought it might be Sam and he'd found her again. Maybe it's Arden.

There had been laughing nights, drinking wine, and crazy fiesta sunsets, dancing by the beach with Arden's friends, and peaceful morning breakfasts with Noah who said Arden was pretty cool. She and Arden held hands when he introduced her to colleagues in the Scripps cafeteria at lunchtime. He told them, "Now, *this* is serious," and kissed her shoulder lightly.

He bought her $500 worth of lingerie. Nothing cheap like Sam would've liked. Beautiful bras and underwear in peach and champagne, silk camisoles in ivory, cotton briefs in sand and ochre, buff and bronze fitted slips and peignoirs made of gossamer wings.

Arden was always a gentleman. He said let's marry next Valentine's Day and she said she'd put it in her planner. When did she feel twinges of change? She went to LA for a conference and he picked her up at the train station, snappy and cranky. Then he canceled one night and admitted he had agreed to see Karen. She was still in his life. One night at the Mustard Bar, he told Molly they needed to slow down.

Gray clouds took over the sky and she had a brackish taste in her mouth at the JCC pool. She told Renata she hated being weak. Renata said, "What's so weak about feeling or wanting something?" Renata towel-dried her hair.

His one son came to visit, and Arden didn't introduce him to Molly. "We were so busy. I'm sorry it didn't work out," he said on the phone. Molly was cooking up some orecchiette with spinach and garlic, Noah's favorite pasta dish.

"Did you tell him about me?" she asked.

"No, I want to wait. You know with kids, they're worried about their own lives. The timing wasn't right."

Why had she opened to him, allowed him into her own son's life?

Another night: His eyes were shut, his hair streaked with gray fanned out on the pillow, his crowning glory, not old-mannish but like that of a young lion king's. They played in a wonderful, sensual way. She circled around the hairs on his chest and jabbed her finger into one part of the swirls. "I want to have a place, a place in your heart."

"That's too much to ask for right now, Molly." She watched his face speak. She submerged under his Prussian blue gaze.

How could it have changed? What had she done wrong? She buttoned her dress and put back the safety pin to keep her breasts hidden.

Arden sat up and his right arm held onto the muscular bulge of his left arm as if for support and he said, "You need to see other people and I do too."

He tries to kiss you goodnight, but it's a lie. This is the slide. Even though you have children, you ground yourself down, even though you remember from Pam your counselor you're not at the bottom of the pool, you can get up again, you are quickly submerging under the whirring blur of the motor into a deeply descending blue.

The plug is your heart and the water is gushing in. No place to swim to but within the confines of the pool. Your legs are like heavy scissors that cut the waves away. Voices grow distant. And after some motions, some flailing about, some lurches for breath, you zoom to the bottom, the cold where no one can reach.

She couldn't sleep for imagining his hands on her. Days she stumbled through as if in shock. She wrote on little yellow Post-its: I'm closing down my heart like a room no longer for rent. On another she wrote: Maybe this is the way men live, moving from place to place, from woman to woman. I made room for you. A longer note, maybe more honest, said: One day he sticks his finger in my vagina. The next day he links his fingers in hers. I have a problem with the geography of those fingers. God, I'd like to not feel this.

The Post-its are scattered like animal feed around her room.

He encouraged her fantasy of living in Ireland for awhile. They read Yeats, Rilke, Donne. He said yes, he felt it and imagined them growing old together. Who was that on the phone? He'd say that was a woman from New York, or oh, he's meeting an ex-lover who went to Morocco with him. There's Lizette. Sorry, Molly, this is long distance. There were lots of women in his life. Once Molly said, "I don't blame you at all. I like women. They're more interesting than men."

Why should he commit? He's attractive, successful, his children are grown, his life is his own.

Molly studied the round bar of soap in her bathroom. *Val* was worn away, *encia* was barely legible. Arden had taken her there the first time they made love. Now her son, his friends, his girlfriend, the plumber were all lathering their hands with the soap, rubbing it. It was obscene. She flung it in the trash basket.

Sensible Renata said he came on full force and then maybe scared himself. The turquoise water in the pool sparkled like ice.

Molly couldn't shake this thing. Melancholy hung over her. Dorie sat down next to her one day at the pool and without greeting said, "See that pale eggplant? Arden's probably a wimp just like that one." She referred to a man with a paunch who was pouring sunscreen onto his bald spot and gently rubbing it in. "He's not even a vegetable," she said, "he's a flounder!" Molly had to laugh.

The kids squealed and splashed. Dorie's girl Livie yelled, "Noogie-butt cannonball" and took a running start before jumping into the aqua zone, splish-splashing everyone. Prime time: another late afternoon at the JCC pool.

Claire said she felt like a bat, navigating by echolocation, but "Sounds like he can talk the talk, Molly, but can he walk the walk?" She was right, her son's girlfriend. Why had she and Noah broken up? Molly liked her so much. Claire brought two iced mocha decafs, and handed Molly one, her treat.

The door had been shut so long. Molly's mistake was opening it a crack.

"So he won't commit," Dorie said, wearing her mod shades. She played with her girls in the shallow end. "He's a successful doctor with lots of social engagements. Just have fun. Love is no guarantee. Paul and I were in love and look now."

Claire remembered Dorie's abandon in the pool. Claire then looked at Molly and said with 16-year-old innocence, "Well, don't let him take advantage of how good you are."

Virginia arrived. She said "Hey now" to Molly and set her stuff down.

Renata said, "He's a society guy. I guess women chase him." Renata looked sorry she had ever introduced Molly to Arden.

Virginia said, "Are you still runnin circles about Arden?" She slipped off her thongs.

"Oh Virginia. Christ. You'd think I was a teenager." Molly fixed her straw hat, embarrassed.

"Well, no man ever wants to be hooked. You don't play the games, Molly. Don't be jumpin up like a jack-in-the-box when he calls. This man wants a challenge."

Claire rolled her eyes as her mother arranged the bag and stretched out on the lounge. "You don't need to play games," Claire said.

"Then where's Noah, today, Claire? Hmmm?" Virginia nearly gloated.

Molly waited a few days, but Arden didn't call. She relented; she paged him.

When they got together, Arden said, "We keep doing this," and he unbuttoned the top of her dress—it was her favorite, a field of English flowers. She trembled. They were alone in his room with its sumptuous red leather armchair, vintage roll top desk, antique map and cherry wood bookshelves with carved wooden finials as bookends. It was such a man's room.

"Skin is the largest organ in the body, you know," he teased.

A current ran through her. "Yes, doctor. Didn't we say we couldn't get physical?" If she could only be stronger. She sat down on a bed of Ralph Lauren sheets. He came close to her. Too close.

Arden said, "Yeah, why can't we—what's the reason again? I'm so attracted to you. I remember your hair, the way your skin smells, I dream of your dresses."

He kissed her nose, her cheek, her lips. Her body tensed. How does a body care or reach out again? How do you trust again? She had to hold back. "I'm not sleeping with you. I told you that." He had carefully stitched brown leather boxes piled on the floor. What was in them?

Arden said, "OK. But if we made love now, it would mean more than before." He rubbed into her. A woman sang like a mermaid or a mythic creature, and the music emanated from his elaborate entertainment center. "How did we get here? Love moves in mysterious ways, like the song says," he said. Molly looked as far away as she could.

She pointed. "Look at that hummingbird. I've watched the sun set on that one branch; the light went from golden to strawberry."

"Oh Molly…I don't know why I stopped the relationship with you, why I…you're a special friend."

"I hate that word."

"How about this? I don't want to lose you, Molly."

Molly said, "Don't call me a friend. You're not my friend."

Arden said, "So what am I? I know. Your guru."

"Yeah, right, my guru. And me, I'm what? Your muse?"

"Yes," he said as he kissed her closed eyes, but Molly's eyes wouldn't stay shut. She stood tall and for a moment said nothing.

"Fuckin leave me alone."

"I can't believe you said that, Molly."

"Did I use the word incorrectly?"

"Molly…"

"I'm getting my purse, Arden. Go back to Karen."

On a scorching July afternoon, Molly was beached at the pool with her hat and book as usual when she saw Dorie. Since Dorie had made love in the pool, she became like flypaper to men, always introducing the group to a new one or flirting with some lifeguard. Today she slurred her words. Her breath smelled like a liquor store. Molly worried for her girls.

"You're looking good there, Molly," Dorie complimented. Molly almost wanted to hear that. Her dreaded birthday was coming. Not that she minded age; she minded having to remember past birthdays.

Dorie wore an iridescent silver one-piece bathing suit with mesh on the sides. Molly had on her plain-Jane, two-piece blue and green striped suit from 1980-something. Dorie walked like nobody's mother. She walked ahead of Molly, the gate to the jacuzzi almost taking out Molly's eye. Molly asked, "How do you make em want you, Dorie? What do you do?"

She laughed a big, Hah. Then she descended into the heat. "I talk cars, sports, I talk dirty." She slipped her body under the bubbles, closed her eyes and said, "Ahhh...." Eyes still closed, she said, "I don't give a shit. That really turns them on."

Molly said, "I'm smart. I can write. I can bake."

Dorie said, "I'd do you, Molly."

"Yeah, but you'd do anybody." They both laughed.

Dorie said, "Just use the word *oral* a lot. Like, I love *oral* expression and *Oral* Roberts. I have good *oral* hygiene. The state of the world is so *oral*, you know." She was delirious. Molly was about to join her and step in the cauldron, as Noah called it.

"Molly, Molly." Virginia called.

Molly couldn't hear what she was saying. Virginia looked like a tomato waving her arms.

Molly opened the jacuzzi gate and walked a few steps to hear.

"Get your buns moving. Our swimming babies are ready to strut their stuff. My Olympic girl and my cute future-son-in-law are about to swim freestyle." She was so sure Noah and Claire would get back together again.

"What?" Something pulled Molly back, like a tug of emotion. She turned around and Dorie was gone. She ran into the jacuzzi and dragged her—bumping and heavy—out. She listened for breathing and didn't detect any.

She pinched Dorie's nose shut with her left hand and lifted the chin with her right as she breathed into her lifeless body. Molly was on automatic pilot.

"Oh, Lord. What happened?" Virginia yelled, running closer.

Molly turned to see if Dorie's chest fell, trying to listen for air escaping from her mouth. She breathed into her again. Her chest rose and fell ever so slightly.

Virginia's hand covered her mouth in horror. "It was so fast. Sweet Jesus. Is she—"

Dorie spit up and Molly wanted to make sure she didn't choke on her vomit. She turned Dorie on her side and swept her mouth clear with her two fingers. More vomit spewed, running along the concrete by the plastic jacuzzi cover.

"But you don't even swim," Virginia murmured. From out of nowhere, Claire, Noah and others appeared to see what the commotion was about.

Molly said, "I used to lifeguard at our community pool back in Iowa. A long time ago."

Dorie coughed and rolled away into the dark recess of her elbow, sobbing.

"Her girls with Renata?" Molly asked Virginia without looking away from Dorie.

Molly could see with her peripheral vision Virginia turn away to check. "She has them bundled up eating Otter Pops."

"It's OK, Dorie. Everything's OK, sweetheart."

Water and vomit ebbed through the grout as if tiles could weep.

Molly thought her birthday was no big deal until the only card she received was from her dentist. At the pool on Thursday Virginia unveiled a little ice-cream cake with candles and she, Noah and Claire sang—Virginia hysterically off-key. Claire and Noah were still dripping from their meet. The tension was incredible. Claire wouldn't look at

Noah. Claire thought of the bitchy girls at her school who made fun of her Wrangler jeans. They all modeled or wanted to model and shopped until they dropped. It made Claire sick. Noah said, "Claire, we can still be friends, can't we?" She ignored him.

Molly hated that stupid word, *friends*. Noah had been mooning around over this breakup, and Molly was wrapped up in her own hurt. But Claire was tough.

Arden finally took Molly for a drink; he had forgotten her birthday. "It's hell with Karen." He looked like he had aged. Then, why don't you break it off? He couldn't or wouldn't. She could see that now. Afterwards, Molly ran a few errands and when she opened the front door, Noah said someone sent flowers. How perfunctory she thought. Leave it to Arden to do the right thing. Her heart skipped.

There were yellow and pink carnations, a bright fuchsia helium balloon, a huge orchid, purple Gerber daisies, pink roses, blowers, a "Happy Birthday" flag. Was this from *him*? Molly opened the card, "You are very special and we love you. Have a fantastic birthday. Love, Virginia, Dorie, Renata and the kids."

They teach you to use a shepherd's hook, to always lean back. Or lay down on the deck and reach. But before they teach you how to save someone from drowning, they should teach you how to laugh at the moon, how to let go of things in your heart not worth holding on to, how to save yourself.

Molly learned to swim when she was 4. Maybe at the age of 42, she would finally learn how to swim again.

The Red Trolley (Virginia)

◆

The red trolley darn near looked like a toy your brother discovered under the Christmas tree. It looked brand spanking new and shiny. There wasn't even gum stuck under the seat. When Virginia hopped on the trolley—she picked it up on C Street—her mind went to nothin and nobody but her little girl. At least for awhile.

What would happen to Claire? None of them women would make the right mother. The Chinese one wasn't even Chinese and she carried too many bags of strange things. What if she opened a restaurant in Virginia's house and forced Claire to bow? The marketing woman used too many big words and had a gap between her teeth which means you couldn't trust that one s'far as you could throw her. What the heck was biotech anyway? None of them would understand Claire the way she did. Claire was a fly girl, her very own, and her music was like one of them gold-wrapped gifts—the expensive kind—from the angels.

Riding open and free like this to Mexico in the middle of daylight reminded Virginia of sneaking off to see Junior Jesus in Covington because it was playing hooky from what you were meant to be doin. Then it was school, now work. Junior Jesus had a vision. He saw the Virgin Mary in a water stain on the wall of the local whorehouse. Quickly a shrine was built, candles lit, a cross bolted to the wall. Pilgrimages were made. Virginia and Sally Kelly took a little excursion one day during math class. Junior Jesus invited Virginia to pray and take what all she had done that was no good and become clean again. He was a brown-eyed chubby thing and it took Virginia all of her strength not to tickle his chin and laugh directly in his face. Junior Jesus carried his pulpit—an empty refrigerator carton painted velvety black with gold stars affixed to it—and told them they wouldn't be seein Mayor Tommy Lee Smith no more because he was so hateful the devil just sucked him away. Meanwhile pretty gals with huge bosoms led pale, puny men in their shirtsleeves up the stairs for heavenly bliss. At least seeing Junior Jesus was good for a couple of laughs. This, on the other hand, was a drug trip, plain and simple. Even if she did get to miss work.

At San Ysidro, the beggar boy sang "La Bamba" louder and louder until she flung some change at him. The routine was: eat at McDonalds, cross the border and take a shuttle to the dirty road, Avenue of the Revolution, where foreigners spoke marbley sounds.

"Kay queery ooh-stay?" they would ask. And she'd think of queers and queens and Vince and how it could all be. A fan stirred the air in the hot store. She unballed the piece of paper from her pocketbook and handed it to the shop woman in the Farmacia. That was easier than tryin to speak their language.

"We don't sell no mothers here," the Tijuanan woman in glasses kindly said. She returned the crinkled paper to Virginia.

Virginia read the first line of her note. "Good Mother Wanted."

She had come to get illegal drugs. The FDA didn't approve them. She'd never be able to spell them fancy names right. But she had forgotten the paper; instead she grabbed the ad. It was the ad for a mother for Claire. Her hands had shook like a drunkard's when she wrote it and her hands went aquiver again. She was sellin her soul, as Junior Jesus used to say. Sellin her motherhood to another mother like it was a big ole watermelon. At a good price too. For nothin.

"You fine?" the Mexican woman asked. "Missus?" The woman squeezed from behind the counter. Truth be known she was bigger than the broad side of a barn, but she had genuine mercy that one.

"Don't you fret 'bout me," Virginia lit a Salem Light. "You think I need these antibuttocks? I ain't sick much these days."

"I be the mother."

Virginia exhaled the smoke through her nose and noticed the gold cross.

"I help you, missus. I have four hijos—boys. One at Hewlett Packard, good company. You know this? Mi casa es muy limpia, no se preoccupe. Necesita ayuda, pobrecita. Esta enferma. I be the madre."

Virginia imagined Claire living with this woman and her coffeebean colored sons eating Taco Bell every night. It wouldn't work. Claire didn't speak Mexican and besides, she hated Taco Bell.

That woman had genuine mercy. Virginia looked with her heart at the stranger. Then, she kissed the Mexican's hand, like a prince would do. It came from nowhere, like the Lord himself told her to do it and she didn't even know it because she was smokin. Darn if her lipstick didn't leave its tracking across the woman's hand so that it looked like the fat woman was entitled to reenter a disco now.

While she crossed the street, Virginia decided to let up on the ads for awhile. The good mothers would be packin their kids off to the beach anyway and the money crank was breakin down. Besides, all of a sudden she had someone in mind.

She heard there were bullfights on Sundays in Tijuana. She'd like to come back for that, but now she had to skedaddle. The shuttle deposited her near the crossing. In the dusty afternoon, she waited for the trolley on the San Diego side of the border. Two Navy men were fighting while the dark Mexicans cheered. A tiny blonde bit her nails and said Please, stop. Don't, Ray. The taller one with the muscles angrily said, "Can't you be decent?" and smashed a bottle of Corona over the stumpy one's head.

The red trolley pulled up and Virginia's car had air-conditioning. Virginia arrived in downtown San Diego near the Convention Center—a big ship of a building—and the new high rises. As she drove north,

Mission Bay whizzed by on the left, then she sped through La Jolla and Sorrento Valley past the merge. Hot air balloons dotted the sky and lifted her spirits. July was her favorite month.

The Lounge Chair (Molly)

◆

Molly wore a jean skirt, muted colors, and at night maybe a light sweater with tiny pearl buttons. She didn't bake much, but she was gardening more and she had made progress in the pool.

She was almost looking forward to the feel of the water this July day. The lane ropes were down. The lifeguard rubbed zinc oxide on his nose and told the boys not to run. While Molly stood by the edge, Dorie called out and thanked her for the journal. Molly had given it to her and said, "Maybe it will help you sort out your thoughts and feelings." Dorie was like a tossed salad, heading every which way. She needed direction.

Molly almost made her goal, but didn't. She was already treading water, but today's goal was the neck. She stood up and searched the pool's bottom. With her eyes pulled down, her mouth torn in a frown, such sorrow ran deep. Molly's face was etched like a negative. But she was clinging to what she had, like a tenacious crab, and that was Noah and Mariah, her garden, her baking, her books, her friends and this translucent determination to swim again.

When she first moved to San Diego from the northwest and saw the women foodshopping in Vons, parading around in their bathing suits, she questioned their modesty. She was embarrassed for them. But now she understood. With Arden, she began to love her body, to show her arms. What a celebration loving a body can be.

She said hello to the woman next to her who was sculpted, always swimming and lifting weights. Now, seeing women work at Scripps reveal their legs or in snug blouses made Molly think they should be proud. They worked hard at keeping their shapes and keeping someone in love with them.

Noah was going to drive them home—with Claire joining them. The clock by the snack bar said 5:23 PM. In the car, the deejay talked about a comet hitting Jupiter. Molly thought of the fireworks Arden and she saw at La Jolla Cove. Arden reminded her of a Jupiter man. She didn't know why.

Traffic to the Del Mar Fair clogged the freeway so Noah drove by way of Torrey Pines Reserve, by the ocean. Cars were bumper to bumper here too, but nobody minded as they could smell the ocean air. The waves were emerald and surfers were changing into their wetsuits under beach towels.

Noah and Claire had broken up and now were repairing their world together. It was tentative, their first date. Molly was proud of Noah. She had told him she hoped he didn't give up on someone just because things got tough.

Noah related how a group of kids were going to Magic Mountain. Claire said it sounded fun. (Weren't pregnant women advised not to ride on the rides? No. She couldn't be pregnant.) There or Disneyland. She said let her know.

They arrived home. "Let's start the barbecue now. I'm starving," Noah said going to get the coals they picked up at Vons out of the trunk.

When she and Claire got out of the car, Molly saw Sam's back.

"What the—" Noah said.

They all froze.

Sam sang along to the song on his Walkman, oblivious to them. "It's OK," Molly reassured. Sam sat in a lounge chair on the lawn cleaning his silver gun with a cloth. He faced the Wright house.

"No, it's not," Noah said.

"Is that him, your father?" Claire asked.

Flashes of silver gleamed in the sun.

Molly said, "I'll go call the police."

Noah said, "There's another restraining order now, Mom. Right, Mom?"

Sam sat singing and cleaning his gun in the sunshine. Molly kept turning behind her to check that he was still there as they ran to the neighbor's.

"Hurry," Noah urged Claire, his arm nudging her forward.

They all huddled in the kitchen of the Ranzlers.

Molly called Arden. His secretary said he wasn't there. How could she call him?

"How can love go so bad?" Claire asked Noah as Molly dialed the police.

Molly was exhausted.

A cop with a New York accent sat in their living room an hour and a half later.

"So he's not in jail?" Molly asked. No. Not again.

"Call me Jake," the officer had said, shaking her hand. They all sat stiffly in the living room on the plaid sofa and loveseat. Claire and Noah were zombies. Molly carried a pitcher of iced tea out of the kitchen.

"Do you want a fresh muffin with the tea?" Molly asked. Her hand trembled ever so slightly as she poured the tea in his glass.

"No, thank you." He sipped it. "This is very fine tea," Jake said putting the glass down on the table.

"What do you mean he didn't violate the order?" Molly asked

"Well, as I got close to the lowlife, he looks at me and he says, '101 yards.' I reread the order. It says he's not to come within 100 yards of your house. I had my partner physically measure the fuckin distance and sure as fuckin shit he was 101 yards away. I couldn't book him."

"What?" Claire gasped, covering her mouth.

"He was polite. Very polite. So I ask him about the gun, what's he got the gun for. He says it looked dirty. 'I'm just cleanin it.'"

Noah looked down. "We got to move, Mom. We got to move again."

"He's not going to make me uproot again. Why do I have to keep running?"

"Then I ask him if he has a permit for this here gun. And he just takes one out of his pocket, all ready, all neatly folded."

"He has a history. I pressed charges. For battery…in Washington. That's why I'm here. That's why Renata, my lawyer, got me the protective order."

"Renata Meyers?"

"Yes," Molly said.

"We grew up together. Renata is your lawyer? No shit…Look, even if he doesn't violate the protective order, if he harasses you, I can take him for that."

"For harassment?" Noah asked.

"It's a stalking law. All I need is repeated harassment with a threat. And let me tell you that little toy he was carryin was a M-1A, 10 pound, 44-inch assault rifle with a walnut stock. You can get one of them for about two thousand bucks used. Probably from Virginia. Out there, they give ammo boxes as stockin-stuffers. Yeah, they probably sell more guns than Big Macs in the state of Virginia."

Nobody said anything.

"I better get going," Jake said as he scribbled on paper. He handed Molly the slip. "You call me, Molly. Anytime. I'll find a way to get this dickhead."

The Good Hearts and the Old Clocks (Renata)

◆

Claire's hand was on the railing of Renata's curving staircase, and she was about to follow William and Jane upstairs.

"Sit down, Claire," Renata requested. "We never have a chance to chat."

Claire exuded confidence. She was 5'6" or 5'7" and carried herself well.

Jane and William scrambled downstairs when they saw their favorite baby-sitter wasn't coming up quickly enough.

Claire did This Little Piggy Went to Market on Jane's toes as William jumped on and off the couch pillows watching. Renata saw the game, her daughter's little toes, then froze. She usually could push things aside that she didn't want to think about, but not this little boy. It would have been a boy and he would have had such tiny, tiny toes. She sent the kids upstairs to practice sharing. The virtue of the month.

Renata sat down next to Claire and bit into a pretzel. She switched tracks, got a hold of herself and said, "Tell me, what's the hardest thing about music?"

Claire said, "Hmmm, I guess it's stuff you know from experience. Like, how to phrase so that you can create a feeling, not by speeding up, but how you make sounds urgent. How you imbue notes. Do you play an instrument?"

Renata laughed. "Piano lessons for ten years."

Claire said, "Oh, I'd love to have a piano. A piano makes a real home. A spiral staircase and a piano."

"And a bit of violin, but I play very poorly."

"Violin, I figured you might play violin."

"And how's swimming?"

"All right."

"With Proposition 13, more funding should be going to girls' sports. Maybe you could even get a college scholarship."

"I'm not good enough," Claire said.

"I bet you are. Well, how's Noah?"

Claire was unequivocal. "We like each other. We're seeing each other again and seeing how it goes." Noah's father holding the gun and Molly's hunted animal expression vividly sprung to life in Claire's mind. Why didn't the police get the bad guys like in the movies? Then she remembered.

Claire was stony faced. "He doesn't want babies."

Renata looked like a deer caught in a hunter's car headlights. "Well, you're young. In a few year—"

Claire licked her top lip. "I didn't get my period June 10 or July 10."

"Oh gosh…"

"Some girls taking diet pills skip their time of month. And Janie Mencken said swimmers can miss their periods for a few months. I feel different. Did you know it when you were pregnant?"

Renata's breathing was irregular. "I'm sure it's the swimming. But if you are pregnant…You're still in high school and teen moms end up poor. And if the mother is poor, the child is poor."

"But I have nothing. Everyone's dying on me, or leaving. I don't want to be alone."

"You're not alone." Renata wanted to reach out but couldn't.

"Babies are precious," Claire said as she munched a pretzel.

"Yeah." Renata tried to forget how precious.

William called for his beloved Claire. Claire looked up the stairs and back to Renata. Renata said, "Go ahead. Claire, I'm here, you know. OK?"

"OK."

Renata slapped her knees and said, "I'll check the mail."

When she checked the mail in front of her house, nothing was in the box, but she noticed the old woman who was recently widowed, a few doors down, was sprawled out in her garden like she was dead. Renata ran past the McDerner house, cut through the Malinsons' yard, brushing by their silver Mercedes and called, "Are you all right?"

"Of course, dear. I'm looking at the clouds," Mrs. Lehavin replied with a European accent, flat on her back, facing the heavens.

Renata let out a sigh.

"Come join me."

Renata was perplexed.

"Come lay down here, right near the bougainvillea. Look at how blue and open this sky is."

"Lay down in your garden?"

"When was the last time you did that?" The old woman's wrinkly blue eyes twinkled with mischief.

"I thought you had a stroke," Renata said slightly miffed as she put her elbows under her head and lay down in her palazzo pants next to the old widow in a splendid bed of color.

"No. When the clock my father brought from Salzburg slows down, well, maybe that's when I'll slow this good body down, too. Not yet."

"A grandfather clock?"

"Nobody has time anymore. I don't care for these digital clocks, just flipping numbers. No sense of minutes, no circular sweep of the second hand, no ringing out of the hour. Time should be good and round. Nothing seems to last."

"That cloud looks like a baby. See it?" Renata pointed.

"Yes," Mrs. Lehavin smiled. "And that one's a house."

"I'm sorry about your husband's death."

"He didn't remember who he was. He had Alzheimer's, you know. How can you live without memory? I told him I was a hooker and he was a bad cop. He became very happy after that."

"And your children?"

Mrs. Lehavin smiled. "Yes, they're marvelous. My eldest son is a commercial developer, very successful. He builds shopping centers and ruins the country. They have two beautiful little girls with red hair and freckles who couldn't care less about anything. And my younger boy just recently married a Parisian model. He's a slumlord in New York. I haven't spoken to him in ten years. Dear, look. Do you see that wisp? Now it's becoming a heart."

"I see, I see."

"Yes, my husband was an Israeli chauvinist, quite handsome. I'm Catholic and Mary watches over me. He fought with Yitzhak Rabin. I was born in Vienna. We came to the United States, my husband did quite well in manufacturing, we raised our sons with no moral character and here we are. Neighbors with the flox, marigolds, geraniums."

How simple this was. Renata didn't need a gardener. She'd ask Molly how to plant. How good it would be to feel the dirt in her hands like now.

Renata said she had to get back and started to get up.

"Resting in a garden of delight..." Mrs. Lehavin purred and in the toasty warmth of the sun, all did indeed seem like a garden.

Renata dusted herself off and said, "I'm teaching my children virtues. Each month, something like truth, forgiveness, citizenship."

"You can teach those things nowadays?" Mrs. Lehavin asked, yawning. A girlish barrette decorated her gray hair.

How do you teach resilience? Renata thought. How do you get back what you've lost inside you?

As Carmella made dinner for the kids, Jake called to say don't wear jeans, get dressed nice. He was on his way.

"Are we going to the opening of the museum show at the Contemporary?"

Jake said, "No, I don't care for jerk off art. But I do like the, what do ya call it, the early *mishegoss* period."

Renata laughed at his cleverness. "A fancy restaurant?" Renata was happy to hear his voice.

"Something like that. Just look nice." When she hung up, she thought of the old woman from Austria lying in a grave of flowers. Was she still there? Something was missing in her life. Or had she forgotten something?

Claire had unearthed a cassette today when she baby-sat. Renata put it on as she dressed. Out the window, in the July dusk, her kids pumped their legs on the swings, eating lollipops, wearing shorts and tank tops and no shoes, and Jake was having fun with them.

She listened to the piano on the Christmas carols cassette that her friends recorded to raise money for Martha's church. Laura Navida's voice was blessed. When Renata heard the final version of "Silent Night" at Thomas and Marta's place on 3rd Avenue near 90th, she could see the windows of skyscrapers, squares of light in the fog and night, like a Steiglitz or Steichen photograph, snow falling up Third Avenue. It was a postcard calling to a quiet place…somewhere sacred waiting for you.

Rings, clocks, hearts, houses. Sacred things that have history. Good things.

The children laughed at the dinner table as they had never laughed before. Jake was entertaining. Carmella carried food in and out of the kitchen.

"Everybody wants what's new, right? New, bigger screen TV, new cellular phone, new car, new toys, it's exciting. It's new. Then new religion, new spirituality because all the new material stuff is nothin but jackshit and we're empty. Devoid. You know what I'm saying?" he asked William with all seriousness, then tousled his hair lovingly.

He could have been speaking Japanese and they still would have laughed.

"This cockamamie virtue thing, Renata. It's great, don't get me wrong," Jake said rising from his chair, "but the Torah and the commentaries have it all there. I ain't callin myself no academic, but that book has been around the block."

"Look what Jake brought me," William dashed from the table and came back with a monster Playdoh set. Jane said, "And he got me a bazing suit for my Bahrbie," and she too dashed to get her loot.

"He doesn't bring flowers or chocolate for me, but presents for my kids," she said half aloud to Carmella, smiling at Jake.

"What do ya wanna be when you grow up, William?" Jake asked.

"God," he said.

"Nothin wrong with setting high goals," Jake laughed.

"Do you want to lay down with me in a garden sometime?" Renata teased as they stood by the door heading out to the fancy restaurant.

"Is that a proposition?" he asked.

She didn't answer.

"You keep doing that."

"This is the fancy restaurant?" Renata was amused as they walked through the temple's doors. Jake said, "Kind of food for the soul."

She saw the ark right away, the stained glass windows, the wooden pews. The rabbi joked and greeted everyone while the musicians played. She read a line in the prayerbook praising God and saying "tenderness shepherded the way."

She had run away from anything Jewish for so many years. Renata was back in St. John the Divine one freezing December afternoon before she moved to California. She and Chichi lit a candle and said a prayer for Lorenzo, Chichi's brother, who died of AIDS. Drugs, Chichi said. She hadn't seen him for years.

The cathedral is the largest in the world, with granite columns, a Gothic nave, tapestries and art, beautiful stained glass windows. Stonecarvers chiseled away at limestone blocks, sculpting prophets in the air. Making holy things out of earthly things. People from all over the world prayed and candles flickered. That majesty of spirit and beauty came back again.

The eternal light in the temple now flickered. She heard South African accents, Mexican accents, Southern accents singing in Hebrew. Jake wore a yarmulke and tallit and sang La Cha Do Di. The boy behind Jake picked his nose. Then the congregation sang Shalom Rav and linked bodies and swayed. She was transported to some place in history and back again.

On their way out of St. John the Divine that icy, December day, Renata read the inscription in the cavernous "Poet's Corner." It was by Walt Whitman, carved in stone, "I stop somewhere waiting for you." So I must stop somewhere? And wait for what was to be? And God is waiting for Mrs. Lehavin, Jake, the children, me, everyone?

The rabbi gave his sermon. Renata gazed at the stained glass windows. Can a soul soar? He quoted Harold Kushner and said, "Encourage is such a good word. Religion should not be in the position of giving answers. It should give us courage to find our own way." He said we shouldn't pray for miracles, but for the strength to live every day, for the ability to find the holy around us—in a sunset, a child's hug, fresh air. Let's pray, he said, for the determination to make miracles happen.

Be thankful, make things happen ourselves. Renata liked continuity, maybe having rituals again. She wanted to get away from the material props, the "suppose to's," the outside life. She wanted to go back, open herself up again to feeling.

What a circular, wonderful thing these traditions are. She was back on Long Island crunching the leaves at her cousin's Bar Mitzvah, she was making apples and honey for the Hebrew school seder…

"I have to piss," Jake said and crouching down, he tiptoed out like an animal so as not to disturb the congregation and service.

They ate sponge cakes and ruggelah and drank punch at the Oneg Shabbat.

"I forgot my watch. What time is it?" Renata asked Jake.

He held up his wrist to her, bending his elbow. She was delighted to see the clockface had numbers and hands and that the face was good and round like time itself.

The 21-Piece Comet Band (Claire)

◆

"Good morning, July 16, 1994. The first fragment of Comet Shoemaker-Levy 9 slammed into Jupiter today. It sent a hot plume into space and created a Gargantuan fireball about half the size of earth." Twenty-one pieces were supposed to hit.

Virginia watched the TV anchorwoman and the views from the Hubbell Space Telescope and telescopes around the world. "You know them astronomers discovered the comet right here up at Palomar Observatory? Your daddy and I used to take you there." She lit the hundredth cigarette of the morning.

Claire ate her soggy cereal and turned off her Walkman.

"The fragments exploded with a force of 200,000 megatons of TNT," the coifed anchorwoman on the news continued as a visual appeared of big red splotches on a blackened screen.

Mama searched for her keys awhile, then snatched her handbag and said be an angel, I love ya to pieces, bye and was gone.

Claire put her bowl in the sink. Mama had a bar of Dial soap floating in a frying pan of water.

The phone rang. She hoped it was Noah. He came into Tower yesterday, his boxers high, his jeans riding low, and they talked a bit. Working in the record store was fun except for having to know all the codes on the computer register at the same time you had a line waiting. Last week, she only worked two nights. She liked evenings because you didn't have to stock as much and people weren't in such a rush.

She told Noah that Talia and Nathan broke up but were together again. One of those off-and-on things. They talked about Arthur Miller's *The Crucible* and witches and being unfairly accused because the manager in Tower clearly eyed Noah. They always suspected high school boys of shoplifting! Noah said he and his mom were OK, there were no signs of Sam, but he was getting a gun from one of the Latino guys, anyway.

It was Dorie. She asked Claire, "Do you believe in fate, destiny or dippity dooh-dah?"

"Maybe dippity dooh-dah," Claire laughed into the phone.

"I need your help today. It's serious."

Claire told her she had to work at Tower. Dorie said, "My brother Ian will pay you two days pay to skip out today, just come with me." Why did Dorie call Claire of all people to go with her to court?

Claire sat a few rows behind them. Renata had good posture. Claire could see by her back. Dorie was dressed in a businessy white suit, but it was way too short. She kept whispering to Renata, nodding and whispering more questions. Other cases went first. A husband who wanted custody of his son but not the daughter. Another case with the wife yelling that her husband has his own software business and hid all the money. "He's self-employed. He makes about $50,000 more a year than that. How can he get away with this?" The judge had to reprimand her while her own lawyer patted her elbow.

Then Dorie's case came up. Paul had cute dimples and said he was representing himself. The judge said, "Let's address the money first."

Renata said, "Defendant is $2400 in arrears on child support payments for minor children, Olivia Rachel Lerner and Natalie Rose Lerner, as provided for in the divorce decree of January 11, 1994."

Paul said, "Your Honor, I've paid for the girls' school and some of the camp costs, but with the economy so bad I'm having problems finding enough contracting work."

The judge asked, "Do you dispute the amount in arrears?"

"No, your honor," Paul said. "But it would be a tremendous hardship for me to come up with that money."

"Do you own a house?"

"No."

"A savings account?"

"Just a checking account."

The judge peered over his bifocals. "OK. I direct you to continue to pay the monthly child support without interruption. And pay the plaintiff $1200 within 30 days and the balance of $1200 within the following 60 days." He wrote the information down. The judge then turned some pages and said, "Next, regarding custody. I have the recommendation from Family Court. Ms. Lerner and Mr. Lerner, you both met with them, I see here, two times."

Paul unfastened something. The paper it was wrapped in crinkled. He arose carrying a huge board. "Yes, but your honor, this is what happened to my daughter in my ex-wife's care." He revealed a poster-size photograph of Olivia with black stitches on her cheek, a purple bruise swelling around it.

"Oh God," someone said. Others started whispering.

The Judge said, "What is that?"

Murmuring from the crowd rumbled and grew.

Claire heard Dorie say loudly to Renata, "She fell, she fell."

Paul was torn. "My daughter required hospitalization. Dorie—my ex-wife—let this happen. She's a negligent mother." The photograph was huge.

Renata stood up and firmly said, "Your honor, this child fell—" she bent to listen as Dorie whispered something else— "at Vons last

November. It was an accident. Family Court recommended my client retain physical custody and-"

Dorie made this wheezing gasping sound. She turned around to Claire and whispered, "He took a picture?" She looked frantically at Renata and back to the huge board. Not a tear lined her face. "She fell," Dorie said angrily to herself.

Claire felt sick.

Paul asked, "Wasn't Dorie even watching her?"

Claire could see Dorie's body quiver and hear hmmmm, hmmm, but she didn't bend. Then she covered her face and the sobbing came and she convulsed into her lap crying. It was heartbreaking. The judge peered over his glasses in Dorie's direction and cleared his throat. A bailiff came up the aisle to hand her a tissue.

The judge ordered that Dorie retain physical custody and that both parties still had joint legal custody, whatever that meant. Many people exited the courtroom. Renata spoke to the judge. There was a brownish spot on the back of Dorie's white skirt as she stood. She had suddenly gotten her period, suddenly started bleeding. It was like her body cried before she could.

"Never before have astronomers seen a comet collide with a planet," an ex-football player newscaster announced on the 6:00 PM broadcast. "Experts estimate this collision might occur only once every few thousand years. Some believe it was a comet like this one which struck earth 65 million years ago and led to the extinction of dinosaurs." Claire was at Dorie's house. She kept thinking of the old Rolling Stones' song, Shattered. Twenty more pieces to come, fragments pelting the planet. And then like the dinosaurs, would they all be gone?

That night, after court, Dorie's brother Ian brought home fish tacos from Rubios for Claire, Dorie, and her girls. Ian said, "Dorie can't say enough good things about you. That Lexxie friend of hers is a flake. Dorie thinks you're level-headed, so great with the kids, a real friend."

Then when Dorie came back to the room, he told them about a fire in Ramona that was raging out of control, that his girlfriend Kate was having a hard time with her boss at work.

Claire used to think that dating and suburban marriages were as boring and predictable as endless lawns. Love was so much more complicated than she ever imagined. Or relationships were. They turned everything all twisted.

Claire had to take the test. The box was coated with dust as it sat on her windowsill since April. Funny, how when she was with Noah on Memorial Day weekend she wanted a kid. So funny, she forgot to laugh! Now two months later, it was already July, she wasn't at all sure.

She wanted to write a song called "Bloody and Yellow Light." It would have 21 different crying, aching sounds, like pieces of a comet exploding. She'd give it to Nathan and Jimmy for their band to perform.

Dorie and Claire watched MTV. Claire helped Dorie bathe the girls and put them to sleep. Before Ian left, he handed Claire $100. "Hey, sport. Sack out here, if you want." Dorie didn't look too good.

When Ian left, Dorie said, "Sorry if I've depressed you."

"It's OK. I'm already depressed."

They listened to kd lang a bit, then watched TV or tried to be numbed by it. Claire told Dorie she thought she was pregnant. It was the worst timing; Dorie was so upset already. Dorie just held her hand and shook her head as if it couldn't be possible.

Claire didn't know why she told her. Claire thought she'd probably be a better mother than Dorie, less irresponsible. Poor thing, she was hurting bad, though.

Then Dorie said, "I thought you guys broke up?"

Claire came home and looked at the pile of motivational tapes she played for Mama. She didn't put on any. They were bullshit, anyway. All bullshit.

Destiny (Claire)

◆

They were getting fried at the JCC pool. Claire kept reminding Mama to reapply sunblock. At least she had gotten her off the Baby Oil. Then Claire saw Noah by the snack bar wearing a plaid shirt completely open and his usual jeans. She went up to him.

"The monster might be back," he said not meeting her eyes. "Mom and I stayed with friends a few nights."

She thought of the Gila monster, a poisonous lizard. "Are you OK?" she asked and touched his cheek.

"This won't work. I love you, but I can't see you right now. I know what you're doing," Noah said.

She wanted to feel his beautiful dark lashes flutter and tickle her cheek.

"Claire, I can't be with you that way. I miss you that way. But it's just stupid. Who ever heard of a girl trying to have a kid while she's in high school? That's what you try to avoid."

"I miss talking to you," she said. She wanted to tell him about history class. Mr. Woodruff, who had a bad case of dandruff, got carried away. He said, "If honoring our Constitution and respecting our President makes me dull, let me be the dullest man on earth." Claire whispered, You are. You are. The cool kids heard and cracked up. But she wouldn't tell Noah now. She watched Molly. "First her feet, then her whole body. That's so wonderful. Look at your mother."

"I can't let him near her."

"Noah-" she touched his arm. He winced. They watched his mother walk through the shallow end. Claire leaned over and kissed him.

"It's really over this time, Claire. Final. I've gotta help my mother." He walked away. That's what they had in common. Mothers who needed watching over. Claire returned to a world of women and wondered why in the world she had to keep losing everyone. Who the heck was watching over her?

Renata appeared in her one-piece tartan plaid bathing-suit.

"Hi Claire, hello Virginia. What's new?"

"Mama was laid off," Claire said filing her nails, stretching her legs on the lounge. What if she really was pregnant? Tower Records paid chump change.

"I'm one paycheck away from the streets. I never did save a thing. I'm worried sick about losin Health Net," Virginia puffed on her cigarette nervously.

"I'm sorry. Can I lend you some money?" Renata said.

Claire was taken aback by Renata's generosity. If Claire was pregnant, who would pay for the doctor visits?

"They had a chance to sell the company and another company jumped on it like a June-bug on a duck. They let us all go. That leaves me high and dry. But I'm here for my swimming lesson. It's like the Foreman-Moorer fight in Vegas. The old guy still had something in him to floor Moorer in the tenth round. I've still got my right hand punch. Virginia Graham ain't knocked out of the ring yet. So I DON'T WANT your pityin around."

Renata looked sympathetic. "Well…You still doing Ocean Aquatics?" She tried to change the subject quickly by asking Claire something.

"Uh huh," Claire said. She could imagine Renata's graceful right arm— nothing like Mama's— lifted and bent as she played the violin, making the elbow absorb hundreds of bow strokes in a single concert...It was like a vibration of strings passed through the bridge into Renata's hollow body.

Renata watched her daughter, Jane. "Jane is over there with Greg." Greg, the instructor, was asking them to think of a cartoon. Had they ever seen puppy dogs digging for a bone? It's buried in a hole so everyone dig, dig, dig. Then Renata shook her head in disbelief. "Look at Molly over there. Look at how far she's come this summer," Renata said and they all watched Molly walk the pool. She was literally taking step after step, moving her arms, as she walked through the blueness.

Dorie and her adorable girls headed their way. Dorie's body was shaped like an eight, like a guitar. A few days before court, she lightened her hair so that it was platinum. Renata told them Dorie did retain custody of the girls after all, but Claire knew that. She had been there that eventful day in court.

Dorie didn't rush over, but seemed dazed and in slow motion. Renata spoke quietly, "He took a picture to use against her all those months later? It's hard to believe. She could have lost those kids."

When Dorie and the girls approached the lounges, Renata suggested instead of swimming maybe they just stay close to the kids today. Maybe it wasn't a good day for swimming.

Virginia said, "You young mothers wear on my last nerve with your frettin and worryin."

Claire thought: Didn't Mama know pools were dangerous? Didn't Mama hear every night on the news a story about a toddler who drowned in a pool? Maybe Renata knew each one of them was drowning in her own way. They all were cranky and Mama was in the worst, pissy mood.

"Come on. Let's us bathing beauties hit the pool," announced Virginia suddenly swallowing down her raspberry swirl, creamy yogurt and rising. Claire remained.

Renata directed, "Freestyle, tag your hand down and backstroke back." Just regular swimming, front crawl, down one length of the pool and backstroke back. It sounded easy enough.

Virginia's kick made huge splashes and she complained about the backstroke. She hated not seeing where she was going. She hated going backwards in life. Her hands entered the water with an exaggerated little pinkie first. Dorie wore goggles and was competent enough Claire thought. Until Renata said after two laps, "Can I give you some criticism?"

"Sure, I guess," Dorie said squeezing her nose to pop one of her ears.

"Let's just do the backstroke and get that down. Virginia, keep your legs close and straight, pointing your toes, and break the surface only slightly. Bending your knee too much, kicking the water up and down, won't give you good propulsion."

Claire expected her mama to lunge at the condescending attitude, but it was like one queen exchanging shoptalk with another.

"Dorie you're swimming too flat on your back. You need to roll more. As your left hand goes under the water, roll to the left. It's like rocking a baby."

"Okay, counsel."

"And don't look up at the sky; tuck your chin slightly. Look at a point that you're swimming away from."

Claire thought of that point —her deserting father, her mother dying, Noah calling it quits with her for good this time. Those cramps. What were they? Pregnancy cramps?

"Focus on that spot," Renata said, "and swim away from it. OK, let's go."

Claire noticed that in the course of swimming, Renata never got her face wet.

Virginia had the coffee perking. Claire was fooling around with the clarinet when she remembered Dorie saying, "Your mother, Virginia, reminds me of one of those low-renters belting out the blues, no offense. It's a compliment really." And Claire thought of her mama telling good, kind Molly at the pool yesterday, "I'm a survivor by choice, you bet your ass," and though she usually didn't curse, her raspy voice suffered the smoke, escaped the burns, but never got rid of the fire.

She was tiring that way, but everyone liked her. And if she played an instrument, she'd be tooting a horn or brass instrument all night long.

Suddenly Claire realized she also played instruments that required strong breath.

I'm my mother's daughter.

Virginia came back from unemployment slamming doors and banging cabinets. She stuffed the mail in the toaster oven, did her "dish warshing" and furiously circled some ads in the paper. She kept clearing her throat, which was gravelly.

Dorie came over. She was less guy crazy. Now she only wanted Mr. Right. She was reading the personals: "This sounds good: Single white male entrepreneur looking for very attractive, fit, upbeat woman 25-35, for walks along the beach, good times."

Virginia said, "Entra-nore means he has no money and is living out of his car. Walks along the beach and good times? None of that costs him a nickel. I swear. He should just say he's lookin for some easy lovin." She poured Dorie her coffee straight from the Mr. Coffee, cigarette ash falling on the table, as Claire practiced.

Dorie retorted, "But Virginia, what's he supposed to do, advertise for a wife and total commitment here? That's not the way guys do it now."

"Jeez. They think commitment is a prison sentence. A man's as nervous as a cat in a roomful of rockers if he thinks he'll be trapped. And if after a few months of datin you even mention the subject of marriage... No gettin around it. You gotta trick him into wantin it hisself. That's Molly's problem. She don't play the game."

Dorie said, "Well..."

Mama softened. "I don't know what I'm gonna do now. No job, no insurance. I'm already charged up on my plastic. Every month the doctor measures the ratio between the T cells to see how my CD4 helpers are doin."

"I don't know that much about AIDS," Dorie said.

"It's not AIDS, it's HIV the virus," Claire emphasized.

"What's a CD4 helper?" Dorie asked.

Claire jumped in, "Let me explain. Molly does PR at Scripps so she got me all this literature about it. Ya see, they count these CD4 cells and if it's 500 cells per cubic millimeter, you have only a 3% chance of getting AIDs within 18 months. Once it falls to 200, you have a 30% chance of getting AIDS. Mama has strong killer cells. She scored even higher than 500."

Dorie drank the coffee. "I knew you were a powerhouse, Virginia. I just don't get it, though. You seem so healthy."

Virginia sighed. "Well you get long breaks between episodes. Then you get the flu or swollen glands or some lady-type infection. Seems like you're just broken down tired, run down, then you feel good again. Go on and read."

"So you don't think he sounds good? Then he says, um, for walks along the beach, good times. Unencumbered please. What does that mean, no children?"

Dorie poured milk in her coffee and Mama said, "Like kids are baggage? You should place an ad like this: Single white attractive female lookin for healthy man any age, any size, with an ego smaller than a freight train. Unencumbered, no penis please." They both giggled. Mama looked at Claire and she continued on her clarinet. Virginia dragged on her nicotine habit.

Virginia stopped advertising for a new mother for Claire. Claire told her to stop the foolishness, trying to speak her language. Virginia said she'd wait for the fall again because good mothers would be too busy with their own kids over the summer and the ads were getting too expensive anyway. I swear, Claire thought, sometimes I feel like the mother. She says if I don't clean my room or do my laundry nobody will want me. Like I was a kid and she can scare me. The next minute she tells me, "Don't you never listen to anybody that says you can't be whatever you want to be when you grow up." Like I was an adult already and didn't I know the world could be mine.

Claire tried to shake open her bottom drawer which was crooked and always jammed. Smoke seeped into the walls, into her clothes. She asked Mama not to smoke in the house anymore. She's sick, but Claire was the one choking to death. Mama said the good part about bein her age was she didn't have to sneak out to the johnny house anymore to light up if she wants to. Claire reminded her about her immune system. She said, "Claire, for the last time. The cough is not due to the cigarettes. Let me have some fun now." And she inhaled deeply and blew Claire an "o" ring.

Noah had been learning about acids and bases in chemistry. Claire felt neutralized, colorless, like a nothing. She had nightmares about Mama rusting. She read everything she could about AIDS and annoyed the doctors. Mama would say, "Claire, honey, where are your manners now?" But Claire thought Mama was secretly proud of her.

Dorie was joking about "Breeder Wanted" when someone knocked at the door. Claire jammed on the darabuka drums, fiddling with the bill on Noah's LA Lakers cap as she figured out what to play next. Her buddy Robbie was into computer music and audited a world music course, part of the ethnomusicology branch at UCSD. He was so advanced. She helped him research a paper on Nigerian kalego. He hooked her up with this guy who played Egyptian darabuka drums. Instead of doing a paper for Mrs. Nielson's class, Claire brought the dude to class to perform. It was awesome.

"Well, I love a man in uniform," Mama gushed to the Fed Ex guy. Claire could make out Dario's brown, busted-up Buick LeSabre parked in front of their house behind the Fed Ex truck. Dario took English as a

Second Language and Naturalization classes at night at San Dieguito Adult School. Sometimes she could hear his Run DMC cassettes, as his window faced her window. He was OK as neighbors go.

The Fed Ex deliveryman had deep acne pits on his face and laughed with a snort, thrown by her mother's flirtation. "Sign here, please, ma'am."

"Ma'am. Now that's nice to hear again. Sure will, sweet thing." Oh God. She actually winked at him. How gross.

"It's from my sister," Mama said ripping the cardboard open. There were papers, forms. "Oh, Lord. My ma. She died yesterday. Our phone was off the hook. When it rains, it pours." Death again running through everything. Claire packed her clarinet and tape recorder. They boarded a plane for Cincinnati that night.

I feel the cold water slither up my legs, my back, and I'm an arrow with my fingertips slicing the blue. Tingling of my shaved legs, my strokes faster, riding up over my bow wave as I'm pulled. Yes. I see the aqua tile gleam, touch the wall, slide down, flip. Bad turn. Noah is gonna beat me. The water like glue now, who am I kidding? I've used all my puff on the first lap, no more breath, my arms making arcs of pain, having to stab the water. I imagine Noah blurring by, laughing at my slow-go.

The plane descended and thumped, wheels skidded, and they throttled back. As soon as they disembarked through that tunnel to the arrival lounge, Claire knew she was in trouble. "High time you got here. Pray tell, look at Claire, so skinny. Has she got it, too?"

"Hush now, Wanda," Mama said, pretending to kiss her sister's cheek but looking at the ticket agent instead. "Claire here is fine, as pretty as a speckled pup under a red wagon and don't you pretend otherwise. She's got a nice little shape, too."

Aunt Wanda picked them up at the airport in Kentucky and drove them across the river. Well they definitely didn't mince words, her mother and her family. Wanda lived in a red brick house in Walnut Hills that smelled like mildew and cat piss. Her third husband had worked at GE Aircraft Engines in Evendale until he left Wanda for a 19-year old. Mama said Wanda was like a snake in a woodpile, but she was going to be on her best behavior.

"You got a tire in your stomach, Virginia? Put on a few, huh? Remember Big Billy Pork Chop?" Aunt Wanda asked as she poked Virginia. Aunt Wanda looked nothing like Claire's mother. She was bony, had frosted, teased hair, a face that looked like it was run over by a tractor leaving lines and wrinkles, a pig-snout and an acid tongue. They sat in Aunt Wanda's kitchen.

"Can't say that I do," said Mama as she bit into a hot dog and forked up some potato salad. The gray cat tiptoed next to Claire's placemat.

"Big Billy Pork Chop tipped 600 pounds at the Columbus Fair. It was in the papers for weeks, he was promoted more than the president when he came south. You remember? You and me were seeing some town boys, don't you remember? "

Mama's intense blue eyes gleamed.

"And remember how," she laughed like a hyena, "Big Billy Pork Chop died that very day, the opening day of the fair. Not good advertising." She cackled like a witch.

Claire's aunt's dress looked like a piñata. Wanda took more food from the refrigerator. "I stopped off at Krogers for you." She spread everything on the plastic flowered tablecloth: fried chicken, hot dogs, beans, potato salad, sweet corn, Christian Moerlein beer, orangeade, milk. "Scoot, Graywolf. Where's Oscar? Claire, have a little beer. It's good for your system. There he is, resting a spell." The brown cat yawned, curled up by the back door. Even with her grandma's death, there was a party. Neither one of them mentioned her grandmother.

When Claire looked in what was to be her mother's and her room she saw a familiar picture, a wedding picture. Sure enough, when she returned to the living room, there it was. Aunt Wanda had placed the same picture of her and her third husband, the German guy, in every room of the house. The same sugary-fake smiles—on a groom who looked so uptight and rigid he could have been sprayed on the picture-frame and on Aunt Wanda with her peanut-face that had been crop-ravaged. Their smiles beamed from the bathroom, the playroom, the living room, the master bedroom and the guest room, their wedding happiness like a white lie.

"Let's go to Arnold's. Come on. Vince liked that place."

Hearing Claire's dad's name unnerved Mama.

"Wanda, don't we need to go through Ma's stuff? Is it still at the home? When's the funeral, anyway?"

"Friday."

"In two days?"

Claire ate at Skyline Chili and tried Cincinnati's famous Graeter's ice-cream and was mostly bored. Her mama talked about working at the Emery Chemical Factory wearing protective glasses and that guy who was all-hands at the Butternut Bread factory. Aunt Wanda reminded Mama about the time her car door froze open when the Bengals played and it was 36 degrees below zero and how that boyfriend of Mama's—John or Steve, what was his name?—was fit to be tied cause he missed part of the game. Oh Lordy, Wanda laughed, and poured more Jack Daniels in Mama's glass.

The whistle blows, take your marks, then bang. Someone breaks. Again we're off. I'm a dolphin diving and I don't let up. I'm ahead, easy arms, good rhythm, propelled. Flip-turn, push off like a catapult. I've got a cramp in my right calf, but I'm going out fast. Through the chop-splashes, breath for air, down again I hear a roar of the crowd. I'm in overdrive and plough up and down the pool. I'm sure my sprints are at least point five faster than they ever were.

Yuk. Claire's body felt saggy. Her stomach was bigger. It kind of heaved out. There was no pool around. This town was dark and humid and if there were a town pool, it'd probably have splintery wooden benches and locker room floors that gave you athlete's foot, cracked coping stones, diseased bugs skimming the surface, loose drain grates that you can't even see and mucky water. And they probably didn't clean their pools as often as in California and the chlorine would be like sting-rays in your eyes. Or she'd get a sinus infection and be out for the rest of the summer.

Where was Noah now? Did he buy a gun? He didn't hang out with the preppies, druggies, surfers or Goths (the pretentious ones clad in all black). Claire couldn't remember his face exactly, but she dreamed about their imaginary baby. It was blue and couldn't get its breath. She woke up in a sweat. She later found out Virginia Graham was downstairs eating Mallomars and asking Molly to be her mother long distance that very night. How weird if Molly became her mother and Claire had a kid with Molly's son. The ultimate California family.

Robbie's face was a little clearer because she knew him for years. He was probably at home doing music or reworking a cable, checking out his telescope or wiring his door so that if his mom opened it while he was out, an alarm would sound.

When they dissected squids in Mr. Genarri's class (the other class did calf eyeballs), their insides looked like a feather pen, all plastic-like, and they had to take their test filling its body with ink, actually using their squid bodies as pens! At least that was more interesting than listening to a conversation about the summer dress sales at McAlpin's and Lazarus that Wanda read about in the newspaper.

Mama and Aunt Wanda returned from the old people's home with boxes brimming. They went through Claire's grandma's get-well cards and birthday notes, diplomas, faded photographs, pressed corsages, and Mama's report cards (Mama got rid of those fast). Wanda started on the carton with old lady brooches, silver coins, a bible, bric-a-brac. Then they both went through the big box of aprons, nylon slips, housedresses, sleeveless shells, stretch pants, church clothes, little hats, brassiere contraptions and girdles, a kerchief, hankies, a couple of car coats and a short black jacket with beaver fur. Aunt Wanda wanted everything, and

Mama said she had no use for none of this crap, except for some of the jewelry. Of course then Wanda said she had to have the pendant and the cameo, and Mama felt pressed to the wall and lashed out that Gram always promised it to her.

Claire sat on the porch in the early evening and realized her B.O. smelled kind of sweet. It was like you dripped the moment you set foot outdoors in this town. She asked them to drop her at a McDonalds so she could get some work done on a book report she was doing for extra credit over the summer.

This adorable black kid, maybe a bit older than Natalie and Jane Meyers, asked Claire if she had a Lion King toy too. Claire said no and he said you can get 'em, just ax someone over there. He pointed to the counter. His mother came over to them. "Hi," she said. "My name is Destiny." Claire told her her name and that she was visiting from San Diego for her grandma's funeral.

She said she had Louis when she was about Claire's age. "Want some?" She offered Claire her fries. Claire had her soda, that was fine, she said.

Destiny had three holes in her right ear; the sun, the moon and the stars lined up in succession. Claire liked that and her name.

"Funerals are hard," Destiny said politely. She didn't have experience. Claire thought this one was easier than her dad's, but she didn't know how she was going to ever face her mother's.

"Someone I know had a boyfriend in the Navy stationed in San Diego. She said it was real pretty, clean and sunny."

"It is. You should visit sometime."

"Me?" Destiny laughed and kept an eye on Louis's progress with his Chicken McNuggets. "Honey, I save coupons for my Huggies and diaper-wipes. You heard of AFDC, right? I wouldn't mind being able to afford my own place period, forget about vacations."

Claire was embarrassed.

"We lived for 40 days in a motel—DSS put us there—with rats and roaches. Them drug dealers and prostitutes outside our window. Louis here started wetting his pants again. I was determined to get us outta there. I got some hours at Wahlgreen's, but it was shit money."

Louis said, "Mommy, look. I'm a mean rat," and he squinched his nose, puckered his lips and rounded his eyes into pellets.

"You ain't no rat. Maybe you are. Yeah, you're a scary rat."

"My mother just got laid off," Claire said and wondered if she could work two jobs or go through her closet and try to sell some clothes.

"That's a shame. Not too much security, now. Even when ya work, daycare eats up like half your income."

"Really. Is daycare that expensive?"

Destiny told Louis his manners were very good and she was going to give him a sticker tonight and read him one extra story. You'd have thought this kid just got a new bicycle, his eyes were so glittery.

She dabbed her straw in her vanilla shake. "AFDC only pays for real cheap, low-grade child care places to dump your baby at, like you're a nothing. I bitched until he got the best teacher there. So I worked my few hours at the drugstore and got my high school equivalency. That was a breeze. Then I took courses at Cincinnati Technical College at night to be a medical transcriptionist, but you can't do nothing if you can't get someone to watch your kid. This doll I met who lives near UC in Clifton charged me only $2 an hour. She saved my ass so's I could go to school at night, but then she was on welfare and needed more money, and one day said she had to up and quit.

Turns out I didn't need her anymore anyway. Louis threw up on me on the way to work one day, then got real sick. What do you do with a sick kid when you got work?"

"Isn't there some daycare for sick kids?" Claire asked.

"No, sugar, there ain't. So's I stayed home, can't say I minded loving my kid up, and the drugstore fired me. Then a snowstorm grounded the bus—man, our winters are getting bad—so I couldn't get Louis to daycare and by the time I did, I was late for my next job at the muffler shop and got my hours docked. A few weeks later, Louie's got a strep throat so the daycare won't take him. My boss is p.o.'d. My credits for the coursework I did are lost. Sounds like one of them TV movies, huh?"

Claire didn't know it was that hard, that what Dorie had to do juggling jobs and kids was so complicated.

Louis said he wanted apple pie for dessert. "Pleeez, Mom. I'll share with you." Destiny was a soft touch and returned with two desserts. Claire couldn't believe Destiny bought her one and she had like no money to live on.

"What do you do now?" Claire asked biting into the turnover.

"I work 20 hours a week at a muffler shop in Over-the-Rhine and I get food stamps. If I take a temporary job for the summer season, like I have a good friend in makeup at McAlpin's, I'll have to reapply and it'll take 45 days to process my application. And if I find a job and I get cut for longer, after six months they cut Medicaid. You're penalized if you try to work more, you're cut from something, so you stay on AFDC. But just so's me and Louis got each other and is OK is all."

Claire didn't catch all of what she was saying, but the next time any of Mama's friends talked about all those welfare moochers and those on the dole, she was going to tell them to shut right up.

"We gotta split, Claire. Pitch that in the trash, Louis. Sorry I talked your ear off."

Claire wrote her address and asked Destiny for hers.

"What for?" Destiny asked.

"Did you get a lot done on your Oedipus report?" Mama asked as Claire jumped in the car.

Claire told her she met a woman named Destiny.

Aunt Wanda said, "Did she try to read your palm?" Mama said she probably knew Oedipus. Both thought they were funny.

"She had a little boy, real cute, and she was on welfare and food stamps. I felt so bad for her."

"Hey, our grandma had eight kids and never took a lick of state money. Her hands were raw with warshin. What these girls have today is a hayride," Aunt Wanda said. Mama said it's a man's world and women and kids get the short end of everything. Claire was furious, but they weren't interested in Destiny or what she told them.

When her mama and Aunt Wanda weren't arguing, Wanda drove like a speedqueen. She told them how she wiggled out of her last ticket by telling the cop she had a bad case of diarrhea and he hightailed out of there right quick. Mama, who viewed machines as aliens in general, especially hated those people who flagrantly disregarded auto safety rules. "That wasn't a full stop," she chided her older sister.

"I stopped, Virginia. What are you all tore up about?"

Both she and Claire's mother spoke like Southern women because they grew up in Greenville, South Carolina and Covington, Kentucky. Their father was originally from West Virginia coal country, and had met and married Claire's Gram in Greenville (pronounced Green-vul). Then Gramps, his new wife and kids moved to Kentucky, then later to Cincinnati, Ohio, just over the bridge.

When Claire met the grandfolks, they had left the Kentucky/Ohio area and returned to live in the south. She was maybe 7. She didn't remember this dead grandmother or Gramps much—their dog clinking on his chain, her grandparents craggy and old, bragging about the sugarberry trees. She did remember gorging on pecan pie, raspberry cobbler and Krispy Kreme donuts, a kid getting swatted for fresh language and how she had to stay dressed up in her "Sunday go-to-meetin clothes" all day, which she couldn't stand.

Claire had never been to Cincinnati or ever wanted to be here. After Gramps died, Gram moved west to Cincinnati again and lived with Aunt Wanda, but Wanda fussed over every little thing. Aunt Wanda put her in a nursing home and fought with Mama long-distance in

California about the expense. Then Gram croaked in this river city, the porkopolis. Mama called Ohio the good-for-nothin, buckeye state.

This was Claire's second funeral. She was getting to be an old pro. Less than five folks there. The preacher said the standard stuff with no meaning. Mama took her to Eden Park afterwards, and they sat on the grass. She and her mama blew dandelion seeds.

"Claire, I'm scared."

"You're strong, Mama." Claire blew hard. The seeds flew.

"I'm scared I said. Scared, ya hear? You think your daddy was the coward? I hated taking care of that sickly, bony man, changing his clothes and feeding him. Ya think I was strong? It was courage, you said? It was shame. I despised the Lord for putting me in that position. Vince is gone, now my own mama, me next."

It was like the funeral was the big storm that knocked over their walls. Virginia's blue mascara ran like rivers. Destiny had looked like a fashion model with her liquid brown eyes shaped like fish, her high forehead and striking face. Why did everyone leave?

It was against Graham policy to launch into a full-scale feelings talk. One time—Claire was about 4—Claire asked her mama why Mr. Nesbitt played with his hoo-hoo whenever you bought gum from him at the Circle K, and Virginia said men had feelings for women, some good, some not right and there were all kinds of feelings and you know some feelings could even get you carted off and locked up if they were disrespecting enough.

"You're HIV positive, dammit. You're not dying!" Claire said. Her feeling could get her locked up now for all she cared.

Some days Claire thought Mama looked beat and the end was around the corner, especially when she'd look worn and weak like the night they flew to Cincinnati. Then other days she'd be fine. The pamphlets Molly gave Claire said the course of this disease was unpredictable. Claire would pretend to herself they were normal, it never happened to their family.

The park was eerily quiet. Death was getting closer. Mama said, "I dreamed of a little village of peace, something very green like this. Maybe someday they'll name a playground for me. Wouldn't that be somethin? To hear a passle of young-ins, as your Gram used to say, a whole bunch of kids playin in the Virginia Graham Playground in a park like this. What could be better than that kind of peace?"

Claire couldn't believe it. Mama had never talked about dying before.

She suddenly remembered. When Dorie asked Claire to babysit Natalie, who had the chicken pox, Claire thought nothing of it. Claire didn't realize, until talking with Destiny, how much Dorie needed her. Then Claire had read the pamphlet Molly gave her and found out that HIV patients can get the chicken pox themselves because their immunity is down. Claire realized she had exposed her mother to it. I thank God nothing happened to Mama, she thought nervously.

That night Claire was too tired to pray, too tired to visualize Mama's immune system kicking butt, strong and pumping. She was too tired to repeat "better and better." In the twilight between being awake and sleeping, she imagined Mama diving from that park off a cliff.

Claire dreamed she sprinkled snow over Mama to make her healthy and clean. Then somehow she was sprinkling ashes over her body and Mama was in her grave.

Claire knew in her heart she tried to steer Mama right. Claire read that endorphins, released when you exercise, enhance killer cell activity and were important for AIDS patients. Mama started exercising a little. Claire got her a guest pass at the JCC gym, and she went once or twice. Mama said she tried the weight room, but there was too much huffin and puffin. She said she didn't care for the metal equipment, but later Claire learned one lady complained because Mama had stunk up the place with her perfume. Women on the Stairmaster were choking for air. Mama apparently shrugged, "My husband said a woman should always wear perfume."

Mama went to the pool sometimes with Molly, but usually swam with Renata and Dorie while Claire practiced in Ocean Aquatics. Claire cautioned Mama, "Watch the sun." She said, "I know, I know."

Good diet was important too, but Mama "will pay you no mind," she said as she devoured a blueberry Danish. She loved her gooey desserts. Finally Claire convinced her to switch from ice cream to frozen yogurt, from eclairs and Pepperidge Farm chocolate cake to Entenmann's Non-Fat Pound Cake, from canned pears in syrup to fresh green melon and strawberries.

Aunt Wanda threw Claire's well-laid plans to the wind. "Have mercy on me, child," Mama said as she sunk her teeth into pineapple custard cake with coconut icing. Aunt Wanda looked on beaming.

All the women in town had metal mouths and missing teeth. They spoke like they were chewing on Gummie Bears. One seemed smart—she had the most teeth. Claire asked her when her baby was due. "Hon, I'm not pregnant," she laughed. Claire could have died of embarrassment.

After dinner, Claire sat on the porch, picking at the mosquito bites on her legs, as the sun went down and the evening stayed sweaty. When the neighbors left, Mama and Aunt Wanda brought their brown plastic cups of rum and coke and sat on the flowered dinette chairs next to Claire. Graywolf nestled by Aunt Wanda's ankle.

"Wheww, she's a wild pony, but a nice girl, Dorie. Claire baby-sits for her little girls. So we walked into the F Street Bookstore, went over to the bumper sticker section and bought one that said (she lowered her voice so Claire could barely make it out) 'Love to Lick.'"

"Virginia, you little devil." Aunt Wanda giggled like she was in junior high. Mama lit a cigarette.

"And I told Dorie, here's what we do. He's not givin you no money for your little girls and goin out there and buyin himself a big ole car, he needs to learn a little lesson. So Dorie and me fixed it to the rear bumper and let him drive around with that for awhile, get all the ladies undone as they pass him on the freeway, right? For two weeks he drove with that on his car. Except I didn't know he had an interview with a lady executive and at the end of the interview she tells him, 'Nice bumper sticker. Don't call us, we'll call you.' And he don't know what she's talkin about until he sees with his own good eyes."

They whooped and laughed for maybe five whole minutes. Aunt Wanda whispered "love to lick" and cackled like a hen. Mama's lit cigarette glowed in the dark. Wanda picked at something behind her eye teeth, still laughing. Mama didn't mention how Dorie had sex with some guy in the pool right in front of everyone. After that day, Claire was honestly queasy about swimming in that part of the pool.

"He ain't even payin for the kids, huh? Well, husbands they come and go. I keep marryin 'em but I sure don't know how to keep 'em." Wanda said. "You sure as heck waited to tie the knot and you couldn't keep that one either."

Mama didn't say anything for a minute, but Claire expected a storm brewing. "Yeah, I waited, but I got me a man who could paint you a dream. A smart one, too, real good lookin. You near wet your pants when you first saw him, Wanda, cause none of your husbands could hold a candle to him. Mama liked him straight off. But Daddy, Daddy the good Republican, kept sayin, 'This boy has no family love.'" Mama had that far-away look she had when she thought of Claire's dad, not the lost look, but the loving one. She continued, "Daddy didn't care one bit for Vince's crazy ideas and politics. They were catching fireflies then, Vince and Daddy. Remember, Wanda? We'd smear them on the sidewalks." There was Claire's mother's joy coming through again.

"Yeah, Daddy made me a glow-in-the dark necklace of them. That's when I was married to Pete. And Daddy'd keep that mason jar of bugs next to the milk on the top shelf." Wanda scratched under Graywolf's neck and he purred.

Claire told them fireflies were actually beetles, but they couldn't care less.

"Not a whole lot a use for those critters these days," Aunt Wanda said, putting a damper on the subject.

"Scientists can now duplicate the compounds that make fireflies glow, by mixing chemicals with oxygen," Claire had to volunteer.

"Is she gonna be a rocket scientist, Virginia?" Aunt Wanda tilted her head and nodded toward Claire.

"I hope so, " Mama said proudly. "We are fire and air, me and this one. We keep each other jumpstarted."

Claire wished she had a necklace of fireflies that glowed in the dark to give Louis. She could imagine his smile. Mama tamped her cigarette with her heel and said, "Well…" her voice trailing.

Upstairs, Claire played the clarinet for awhile. What music would she remember when she grew up? What music would define a person or moment? What music would Mama be?

Claire taped Mama and Wanda's conversation (they thought Claire was in the bedroom). Then Claire raced back upstairs. You could hear Mama's laugh every once in awhile. Then she rewound, erased all the talk and just kept Mama's laugh. Claire had started this project with Virginia's snore and her singing in the shower so at least Claire would have something to remember her by. "Virginia Graham's laugh," she said into the microphone and shut the machine.

Claire guessed she should be more grateful, as Destiny was. The room was so hot; it reeked of cat. She tossed and turned in bed until 1:30 AM. She called Talia long distance.

"What's the deal? Do you know what time it is?"

"I'm sorry, Talia. I don't want to be pregnant!" Claire said.

"Did you take the test?"

"I'm afraid to. What if I am? I can't raise a kid!"

"Claire, let me get this right. You buy the test before you have sex. Then you're scared to take the test because you might not be pregnant. Now you're scared because you might be?"

Claire said, "I must be an alien."

"Call me tomorrow, girlfriend, when I'm awake."

I start slow. The water feels like warm piss and I hit the lane rope. But you can't blame the equipment, the umpire, the weather, like in other sports. It's just your arms aching, your breath burning, your thighs fighting the soup which has thickened now—to kick, to propel yourself further. And it's your body alone and gallons of chlorine blue. Turn. Uh-oh. Feeble push-off. I'm losing. Noah is gone, Mama is close to dead. I'm a loser in this swirl of water. My body not just 2/3 filled with water, but waterlogged and bloated with water. It's in my lungs, it's ballooning me up, slowing me down.

In the morning, they packed to leave and Aunt Wanda said the rain was a frog-strangler. Wanda said, "You still carrying Daddy's blue Samsonite around?" but she didn't offer to help carry the heavy thing. She was slinking into the driver's side. The rain didn't let up. Mama and Claire sat in the back and Mama said open the window, we need air back here. Cincinnati had so many old buildings and seemed industrial and dark to begin with. With the heavy downpour and late afternoon approaching, their whole world seemed damp, sticky and depressing. Virginia made a big stink about wearing lap belts and signaling and telling Claire's aunt to slow down for Jesus sakes.

Aunt Wanda drove to the airport with the windshield wipers on "full speed ahead" and Mama and Claire squirmed uncomfortably in the sticky back seat. Aunt Wanda remarked, "Look at that. Those kids in front of us." Virginia and Claire sat high in their seats to see the teenagers in the mint-green Monte Carlo one car ahead. He had his arm around her, her head on his shoulder.

God, what if I can't get Noah back? Claire thought.

"Lovebirds. They're cute," said Mama. "What are you fixin to say?"

"They're not worried about seatbelts is all. You don't see that kind of thing anymore with people sitting close."

"Now they got His and Her airbags," Claire volunteered.

"Right," said Aunt Wanda, thinking Claire was siding with her.

Mama was getting revved, Claire could feel subtle changes in the air.

"Virginia, what's the point of this obsession with protectin yourself? I mean, whether it's a car crash or we're hit by lightning or get the cancer poison, we're all goin anyway. Why don't you relax and quit pesterin everyone with your rules? Rules don't apply when you're dyin. Besides you don't even have a job."

"You tryin to give me my death of cold back here? Roll that window up," Virginia said. But she hated confined spaces, no air. Aunt Wanda rolled the window up, and the bit of fat under her arm jiggled like a chicken's. Actually, aside from her vehicular madness, her mama didn't live by rules at all.

When they reached the terminal, their bags on the curb, Claire kissed Aunt Wanda with a quick throw-away peck. Mama leaned close to the window on the driver's side and slapped Wanda's face. The air crackled.

"You old fool. No wonder they leave you and you're barren as the desert floor. I live by rules because I want to live as long as I can—to take care of my daughter. And I also happen to like this here life. You know, I don't give two hoots and a holler if I never see you again. Thanks for the hospitality now."

And just like that they were heading back to San Diego.

Destiny and her sun, moon and stars reminded Claire about being grateful. She was grateful for whatever days were left on earth that she could spend with the woman who was trying to convince the ticket agent that their oversized Samsonite was a carry-on and would fit fine under one seat, the dark haired quality control supervisor with orange lipstick who came back with a Snickers bar and a movie magazine, the woman who embarrassed Claire no end by saying, "I just love your face," as she squeezed it tight. Oh Mama, hold on now. Our plane is about to take off.

Act III

(August)

Feeding the Ducks (Renata)

◆

Virginia, Molly, Dorie, Renata and Claire were supposed to meet at Seaport Village and pretend they were tourists—Dorie's idea. Dorie strapped a Nikon around her neck and wore Bermudas. Virginia and Claire were there. Molly was late. Powdered light shimmered off the harbor.

They made small talk, catching up. Dorie said sorry about Virginia's mother's passing and asked about Cincinnati. Dorie said she has enrolled in college again, about time really. "Girl, you're gonna do great. Good for you," Virginia enthused and hugged Dorie's shoulder to her. Renata said congratulations.

Dorie said, "I have to move on with my life. I can't keep looking for that white knight anymore. Right, Claire?"

Claire looked nonplused. Virginia said, "Let's hope he darn well won't have a pierced nose and a whole mess of pierced parts like that kid Claire has picked up with."

"Mama, I don't want to hear this," Claire said.

"What kind of name is H. Byron anyway? What do you call him, H?"

"I call him Byron."

"And why does he gotta have a hole put in everywhere? He's got a hole in his head, that's for sure," Virginia shook her head in dismay. "I hope you're not canoodling around," Virginia said. Claire's always been headstrong, doing what she wants no matter what people say. Even at the age of 3, when they lived in an apartment complex in Clairemont,

Claire drove her tricycle right into the pool. Claire was always attracted to pools.

Claire knew if she dated both Noah and Byron, girls at school would call her a "ho." Claire refused to confess to her mama or anyone there that she and H. Byron were just friends. She decided to let them think what they want. It made her sound more popular anyway.

Dorie brought icy cold juicy grapes for them to munch on. Twelve-forty. Where was Molly?

Renata's cell phone rang. Molly was on the line. "Molly, aren't you meeting us at Seaport Village?"

"Sam's outside."

"What's he doing?" Renata froze.

"He has this electric car. It's one of those Radio Shack toys with a controlling device and he's making it go around my yard."

"OK. I'll call Jake."

"Renata?"

"Yes, Molly."

"Call him fast, OK?"

"I'm really worried." She told them about Molly's call. They talked by the kite store.

Claire asked, "Why doesn't this guy leave Molly and Noah alone?"

Virginia was feeding the ducks. "Claire. Look." She said to Claire, "The mama always feeds the ducks. You notice that." Claire and Virginia threw bread crumbs at the water like confetti at a party.

Molly suddenly appeared.

Everyone stirred. Molly announced, "They picked him up. Just like they were supposed to. Everything according to plan. Good old police, good old courts, everything like it's supposed to be."

Renata said, "Are you all right?"

Molly said, "Of course."

They all watched the sailboats and Navy ships in the harbor. Dorie and Molly searched for the boats with poetic names. Meanwhile, Claire sidled up to Renata and whispered, "Renata, I think I'm really pregnant."

Renata grew cold. Renata grabbed Claire's shoulders and shook them lightly. "Kids cost money—for preschool and daycare and doctor bills. Having a child is expensive."

"I don't know if I have a choice now."

Renata looked in Claire's eyes and Claire looked in hers and it was as if Renata saw for the first time what Jake called "a spark of a soul."

A few feet away, Dorie and Molly discussed names and words. Dorie said to Molly, "I write everyday in that journal you gave me. I keep it in my bag, right here." Dorie's 75 bracelets jangled as she took out the journal.

Molly said, "Read me something."

Virginia, Claire and Renata were receptive, too. They ate fish and chips on picnic tables, the harbor and boats behind them, and listened.

The waitress asked Dorie if she wanted anything else to drink.

"Not even Sex at the Beach?" Virginia teased.

Dorie said, "No more of those." Then she read quickly and undramatically, "My friend Claire and I went on a sacred drive to Lou's Records then to Papa Gus's for Caribbean food, then to look at toe rings."

Virginia looked at Claire, "Don't you even think about it. Rings go on fingers. That's it."

"It's not rings. I want simple things that only money can buy. I can't wait for luck. Or a guy. I've got to get my life back."

"How do you get it back?" Renata asked. "That's the million dollar question."

"When you read that," Virginia said, lighting a cigarette. "I was thinking about my own mama. She did the best she could. I think she looked on me as a good daughter. And on my daddy as a good daddy, and

Wanda, my sister, well, as a big mistake. And we all went through life together after all. Like Claire and me will I guess…"

As they wound their way on walkways by ponds, fountains and colorful landscaping to the parking lot, Dorie told New York-born Renata that the restored Broadway Flying Horse Carousel was originally from Coney Island in New York. Virginia said, "Isn't that pretty. Listen, Renata, they cut my insurance. Can they do that? I've got another yeast infection."

Claire said, "Mama gets swollen glands, a cough, a yeast infection, but then she's fine."

Virginia said, "Honey, I need to ask Renata 'bout the insurance now."

Renata said, "They can't discriminate."

"Renata, dear, the job has done gone. The company sold. The company dropped the coverage."

"I think there's a 60 or 90 day time you have to get Cobra or some other coverage. Call me later at the office."

At the office, Renata called Jake right away. He said he arrived at Molly's house, but nobody was there. No, he didn't pick Sam or anyone up. Strange.

Renee Johnson came in and updated Renata on her own divorce. Michael wanted her to waive spousal support, was offering only a few thousand a month for child support. She looked through Quicken, did some quick calculations and realized she would lose the house.

Outside her window on Sixth Street in downtown San Diego, it was snowing. Renata called her parents for the first time in months. She could picture Mother saying, "Be whatever you want to be," while her pearl necklace almost choked her.

"Dad, it's Renata."

The Best Thing Off the Menu (Claire)

◆

Renata later said she had dreamed that her kids' clothes were scattered in the pool. Socks floating, her daughter's white patent leather shoes on their side, William's orange soccer shirt like a flare bobbing in the chlorine.

On this crystal clear day in August, Claire went to the JCC to swim, then for a conference with the swim coach and she intended to go to her summer job at Tower Records. Virginia was doing temp work and hating it, but as long as Claire dropped her off at work, she let Claire have the car. Virginia Graham was letting her drive!

Dorie's little girl Natalie ran to Claire, her baby-sitter, and told her why they needed to put pennies in Mr. Potato Head. That was her bank and if she went potty today she'd get another penny, a reward for being all grown up. Pretty brown pennies dinging in the plastic gut of the funny-faced toy she carried. Meanwhile, Dorie said hi and walked her feisty Olivia over to the field.

Claire was thinking about Noah, how he was strong-willed, stubborn and grounded to earth. All in one key. As if seven days of the week could be all the same rigmarole, the steady shoveling, *pah bum, pah bum,* of playground sand. You'd think he'd play the drums, be the assurance of the heartbeat, but he's a surprise. He's a jazzy improviser, like all guys she guessed.

"There's Mike Avery eating a Pop-Tart," someone said.

Claire could play you a riff for every shade of blue: cerulean, azure, Dresden, aquamarine, but she couldn't describe this day's sky. It was like a glide in the pool: pushing off hard then tapering down into stillness, then too much stillness, no leg or arm action. Too quiet.

She looked up at the palm fronds. She had gone to the pool: long course, 50 meters, 8 lanes. She wore molded ear plugs and goggles and felt like a dolphin. She had even bought a white bathing cap that reminded her of a condom joke every time she put it on. But once she was deep into the blue, swirls of light reflected through the waves and she swam through the hum.

Sometimes when Claire swam she felt like her mama on vacation in Miami Beach in those shaky 8 millimeter home movies. Virginia push-pulling with her arms, kicking in flutters, then turning to wave at her dad, her dad who sizzled like a lobster that very afternoon and had to stay in his room beached on ice, sending Mama out for more Solarcaine.

Claire did the front crawl, somersaulted into a flip turn, pushed and, with arms overhead, arrow-like, she glided. Someday she'd figure out how to push off and roll onto her front in one fluid, streamlined movement.

Once in a while, she floated. It's natural she learned in Mr. Genarri's class. We float because our bodies have less density than water. The wet buzz in her ear sounded reassuring like a hymn, but not for long. Then the bad stuff came. Why didn't Mama tell her how little it takes for us to drown? Why did she make it all look like a piece of yellow sponge cake with goopy frosting? Like you go bob, bob, bobbing along, smiling for the camera. Like everything was fine.

Some days shook them and everything they held dear. Like the day in Eden Park in Cincinnati when Mama lost it and talked about her death like it was around the corner. Or this day in August that Claire would never forget midway through the second session of camp. They followed the stream of moms and kids from the parking lot. Sweet Natalie Lerner with her purple plastic sandals, ruffled summer dress and beaded bracelets, laughing as Claire swung her hand, back and forth, like a swing.

Dorie wore a baseball cap, daisy earrings and yellow minidress. The white cumulus clouds luxuriated in the endless blue. For awhile, the three walked. Natalie spoke her coppery words that pinged off the cars. She spoke in child time, which is like the Australian Aborigine's dream time when Ancestors moved on earth and when nature, land and spirit were one. Claire's English teacher said it's a mythical time, when life seems good and immeasurable. And the chlorine from the pool wafted gently through the air at 8:45 in the morning, that summer smell suspended, everything motioning slow.

Dorie said she'd be right back. Another Jeep Cherokee's door shut and a woman said, "We missed his swimming lesson yesterday. How are you? Did Isabel's fever go down?" And 3-, 4-, and 5-year olds with Barney knapsacks, Lion King and Ninja Turtle lunch boxes gently spilled out. Clad in their bathing suits, their moms in shorts saying, "Matthew, now." Carpools of curly heads and ribboned ponytails, kids heading for the swings or the slide, dropping beach towels and then retrieving them, before they got to their camp rooms and circle time.

Molly was by the pool gate and waved. She wore a khaki skirt, a bodysuit and sturdy sandals, as she let Noah in. Noah looked at Claire and then quickly away. Molly has an arrangement with the marketing department at Scripps Hospital so that she can come in 9:30 every day.

Claire has an arrangement with herself not to care about Noah, but she wanted to run into him. She knew full well this was the time he swims.

Renata is opening the door of her forest green Lexus now and sliding out slowly, almost imperiously. Natalie talks to Arielle Berman in front of room 8, which is in the green trailer with the pink door. The trailers were painted kid colors by a few of the parents over the break and reminds Claire of Playdoh.

Renata is brisk and elegant in a slim navy dress as she waits for Jane to lock the car-door. Her older boy in private school looks more like his dad, but Jane is dark-eyed and dark-haired like Renata, with good manners. Renata pops the trunk to get Jane's stuff and then Renata freezes with her slender fingers still raised on the trunk's hood as if she is gripping the upper lip of a beast. Claire can see her throw her head like a proud horse, almost flip the wisps of her brunette bob and then Claire sees who she is looking at.

Michael lurks somewhere waiting for her. He gets out of his Volvo. It looks cold, gunmetal gray and he approaches her and Jane. They had recently separated but everything was cool between them.

Renata scoops up Jane in her jean shorts, a red and white striped top, white socks and white hightop sneakers. The parents speak a bit. But Claire senses the trill, the first measures of a darkening crescendo. Something is terribly wrong.

Her jawline squares while he insists. He speaks more. Then Renata takes out the pink knapsack and slams the hood down. Michael points to where Claire is and challenges Renata. She looks fearless and solid, as if she were saying the answer is non-negotiable.

Daniel the gym teacher says, "Yo." He is a triathlete with blond hair and an earring, already on the top stair to the office. He's an up-guy, forever in motion. By the time Claire looks back to the parking lot, Jane is in her father's arms, darting questioning, nervous looks at her mom.

Michael steps back with Jane in tow. It's like Michael is going in reverse, taking three giant steps in the wrong direction. Some mothers sense something not right. Claire would later be a counselor to these kids and they all had stories about this day. David Street, decked out in Mickey Mouse ears, stops in his tracks. Donnie, almost nineteen and now on the maintenance crew, has just cut the pipe and holds the new fitting for the sprinkler in his hand. He too watches. Then Jane flings her arms toward her mom and Michael pivots Jane away.

Renata's back is to Claire, but her hands, polished and proud, seem to be reasoning with the air. One hand's fingers spread with palm up, gesturing to the sky like "what is this?" Then shoulders hunched up, both palms upwards like "I don't know what to do. This is crazy." And then palms facing each other as if to clap but instead defiantly slicing the air, "You are not going to do this, you are not." Michael's arms locked closer around his daughter, enacting a force unyielding.

By this time, Maura Greenberg and Janie Cheng quit talking a few yards away. Jane's cries swell, "Mommy, Mommy" and Michael inches a step back, holding her captive. Then more moms, holding infants, some in workout clothes, some dressed for work, walk cautiously, looking. A blonde toddler in her JCC camp shirt hides tentatively behind her mom as her mom pulls, "Come on." The Russian woman who has the 2-year-old class perches outside the yellow door in the purple trailer.

Claire yanks Natalie and they walk closer to the fence where Claire hears Michael plead, "I have a right to see my own kids. They're mine too, my kids." His voice peels with emotion. Jane is screaming, swinging out to reach her mom. What could Claire do? Her heart shakes in tremolo.

Molly takes charge, "I'm getting someone." Claire didn't even know she was behind her. Claire thinks Molly means the director. But she comes back with the black bus driver and a muscular guy from the workout room and they all stand close.

Jane is by now kicking and flailing and hysterical, shaking her head back and forth so violently her blue flowered ponytail holder flies off and the vein throbs in her forehead. "Look at Jane, Michael," Renata says coldly. "Look at Jane." But she doesn't grab her daughter as Claire thought she would or maybe should have. The muscular guy steps forward and then stops.

Jack, the maintenance man, looks up from raking the new sand-spread, squints and moves the toothpick to the other side of his mouth.

Mom-myyyy, Mom-myyyy, her cry tears at you. More kicking.

Mom-myyyy.

He steps back again and Claire's heart beats wildly. Renata doesn't move. Michael wasn't far, 20 or 30 feet at most, from his car. He holds Jane tightly to his chest.

Suddenly he relinquishes his hold, almost dropping her.

Jane folds into her mother's arms; her sobs sound like the yelps of Rubio's beagle after he was shot near Claire's house.

They all let their breath out.

Renata rubs her daughter's back and Jane cocks her head on her mother's shoulder. And then Renata walks—her gait is purposeful—toward her daughter's classroom as Jane hiccups *hiih-uhh, hiih-uhh.*

Michael follows and then he fastens onto a corner of Jane's striped shirt. Renata says, "What are you doing?" It's so strange. He won't let go as she keeps walking with a regal dignity, striding on.

Michael trails, clinging to his daughter's shirt hem, as Karen Cohen asks Renata loudly, "Are you all right?" Renata says it's OK. The preschool director appeared and announces that she has already called the police. Renata nods and slides soothing words to her daughter in her unwavering alto voice. The three of them enter the red door in the blue trailer, the class with curtains in the window.

They all stand—mothers and counselors and children and Claire—in the dry, San Diego sunlit morning. Claire hears Dorie's shoes squeak up to her and Natalie, as if walking through mucky water. Her voice sounds like exposed wires, "What was that?" Natalie says nothing as if she knows something major has happened. They gather their strength. Tamar Shapiro, who works as a counselor, puffs out her tie-dyed shirt as if to let in air and mumbles, "Was he going to *kidnap* her?"

Olivia says, "That Daddy was bad. Dads who live with Moms are bad, right, Mommy?" Dorie says we'll talk about it later. She brings both Olivia and Natalie close to her body.

Molly bites her index finger. Her other fingers look like a crab roll. From Claire's angle, she almost believes Molly is sucking her thumb. Claire wonders if Molly is in shock.

There's a catch in the air, as if a zipper got stuck on the wind, or a crosscut saw rode to-and-fro, *hiih-uhh, hiih-uhh.* Claire asks, dazed, "Is that Jane still crying?"

One counselor goes upbeat with a fake voice, "Where are our ducks? Good morning, room 6." And the ducks and dolphins and fish trudge away from the adult spectacle and return to their world of talking trains, face-painting, poo-poo jokes and jostling to be first on line to the pool. The mosquitoes, room 7, buzz with anticipation. The petting zoo was coming today.

A kid in a Batman cape yelled, "Hey you. That shovel is mine." Meanwhile, Molly, Dorie and Claire walked to the parking lot. Molly held back as always, Dorie kept saying, "I can't believe it." Claire listened hard as if somehow hearing everything better, everything would make sense. Little Jane's turquoise lunchbox had sprung open. Her tuna sandwich, cut in triangles and wrapped in plastic, was splayed, the plum had rolled a few inches away and the carton of apple juice lay on its side next to a wad of gum waiting to be crushed or found. "Jane's..." Dorie said, kneeling to pick up the lunch box. Molly rubbed Dorie's back reassuringly. Claire stopped for a long minute, waiting for someone to explain.

Renata came over and said, "Michael called and wanted to see the kids this afternoon, but we had plans. He got angry, really angry. He said you can't tell me when I can see my own kids." Renata picked up the sandwich and juice and put it back into the lunch box. "You know Michael always insisted on buying me the best thing off the menu. Sometimes I didn't want it. I wanted something else." She picked up the dirty plum and added that to a meal Jane would never know.

A police cruiser pulled up. "You OK, Renata?" Jake said, bolting out of the car. "The kid OK? Is it Janey?"

Renata must have dropped her purse and briefcase somewhere because the last they saw, Jake's arm was around her and the very reserved lawyer walked away clutching only a turquoise Barbie Ballerina lunch box in her hand, its clasp re-shut tight.

Blue Angels (Claire)

◆

It was the 40th anniversary of the air show at Miramar Naval Air Station. Saturday, August 20, 1994. Noah and Claire decided to get back together. "On a trial basis" Noah said. Claire agreed they'd see if things could work. They were entranced with the aerial show and viewed the civilian and military flight demonstrations as they zigged and zagged with explosive sound. This was the sensation they were after: a flying low and building straight up, something like music that made your heart rumble, something that exploded and bravely lit up the sky. Ahh, a lady gasped. Hot dog, a sailor said as a jet-powered vehicle blazed across the flightline. It was better than fireworks.

Hundreds of aircraft were also on display on the ground. People milled around. Some managed to get autographs from the pilots, others bought souvenirs. Then one would hear the roar and shield his eyes and look up. Many came prepared with beach chairs and hats and coolers and binoculars and cameras. A few brought earplugs. It did get loud. A fat bearded guy smoothed sunscreen on his daughter and everyone knew this was one of those events that reminded you why you lived in San Diego in the first place.

Noah mentioned something about the vote. Her whole school had voted on whether to have condom machines in the high school. Noah asked Claire how she voted. Claire said she was for them. Noah laughed. He said he believed in having vending machines of any kind. Claire laughed and punched his shoulder. Noah wondered if her vote meant she let go of the idea of having a kid? He didn't get it, I mean, she was so together except for that babymaking stuff.

Those who chose the freebie route—who didn't want to pay the $5 for grandstand or $12 for box seats—craned their necks to watch the loops and acrobatics. The slightest breeze blew over the tarmac, but it was warm. By 2:00, many sat in the shade of a B-52 bomber's wings.

The planes twisted and turned as the pilots did low-to-the-ground aerobatics and the coolest stunts. They dived, looped, scooped, mounted, twisted and plummeted fast. It was impossible. And just when the crowd was oohed and aahed out, the Blue Angels taxied into position. The popular squadron flew new McDonnell Douglas F/A–18 Hornets, fighter/attack aircraft.

Noah said that one Hornet cost $18 million.

Claire read in the Union-Tribune that one reporter hitched a ride in the F/A-18 Hornet and went faster than the speed of sound. Did that mean if she yelled Yahoo, her voice was lost? Or did it echo much later? Like way in the future somebody on a farm somewhere in China would hear the reporter's Yahoo coming from a ditch? If you traveled faster than sound, were you ahead of music? Did you accelerate and the universe slashed open and then there was nothing? Maybe this is what death was, what Daddy heard. The reporter said when they flew to 6.2 Gs, whatever Gs were, she felt like her body was sucked down a hole. Daddy must have felt like a piece of dirt fiercely sucked up in a vacuum bag...and then like a cotton wad of nothingness.

It seemed like people came from El Cajon and Lakeside, Coronado and Bay Ho, North Park and Logan Heights, to view the aerobatic feats of the Blue Angels, the Navy Precision Flight Team. They were known for their trademark loops and their C130 Hercules transports. A red-headed guy with a ruddy complexion and yellow teeth stood next to Noah and proudly proclaimed, "Slick. These new Hornets. They just keep getting better, man." The Blue Angels tore up the skies. The audience applauded wildly for the daredevils, their very own.

Claire was holding Noah's hand. She said, "Virginia is getting worse. She lost her job."

"Yeah?" Noah said.

"And now her health insurance." Claire followed another precision flight carefully. *Maybe one day she would fly with Mama into the very mysteries of life. She could see Virginia Graham as a tough broad version of Amelia Earhart saying, "Shoot me off now, honey. I can't wait all day." And they'd go into a torque roll, a tail slide and a spin. And then Claire'd somehow understand heaven and love and living and dying.*

Noah suggested they buy Gatorade. Claire whished the liquid around her cheeks like mouthwash. Sugary and thirst-quenching. "I had to take Mama back to the doctor. She had a little relapse. Her CD4 cells fell from 200 cells per cubic millimeter. They say she has a 30 percent chance of getting AIDS within a year."

"Gosh."

"Yeah."

Noah said, "Wow. AIDS and braces. Two things I never wanted to get."

Claire appreciated that. She certainly didn't want to dwell on her concern. Besides, Mama would fight it. Then he talked about Sam stalking his mother, how he didn't get the gun yet, but he wasn't as worried.

"Do you ever think of your father in a good way?" Claire asked dispassionately.

Noah said, "That's a waste of time. He ruined all the good stuff, ruined everything. Did I tell you my mother is whistling these days? She never whistles."

"Your mother, I really like her."

"She likes you, too. She's stronger than most people see. Over 100,000 people here easily," said Noah, doing an estimated head count.

Saturday at 6 PM. there was a twilight air show for the first time on the West Coast and the largest twilight show ever in the United States. They had to enter via the South Gate, on Harris Plant Road.

But Claire was sticky and tired, so at 4:30 PM. they left.

They drove to Talia's house. She lived past San Dieguito High School and Chapel by the Sea. Right on Windsor, past Ida Harris, right on King's Cross, and hers was the pretty mint house in a sea of Tudor Browns. Everyone on their street had a mailbox jammed into a bucket of flowers. Claire needed to drop off the earrings she had borrowed months before. But Talia wasn't there. She was accepted to a college in Florida and she had to leave next week. Her mother said she had so many last-minute errands. Claire thought: another one leaving me.

Noah and Claire rented a video and went back to Claire's house. Mama was out for a few hours. Mama said that movies that made you think were too much like what we lived. She wanted spectacle and violence and drama on the high seas and entertaining epics and thrillers that sprawled the globe. Who wouldn't want to be taken away?

But Claire wasn't after exotic travel and fast action. She was hoping to figure out things. Like, how come after she got drunk in the field, major keg night they called it, did she end up puking on her Keds along with everyone else? She was neater than that! Or how can sex be like running or swimming, just an action, when it made you feel confused? Or about childbirth, for instance. Was it as scary as Dorie's pictures in the photo album? What if the baby's head got stuck like a cork? Maybe instead of being a marine biologist, she'd help babies not get their heads stuck. Or she'd help women with HIV. She had taken out enough books from the library to be an expert by now.

The thought of her being pregnant had become too real for Claire to even entertain. No period on August 10th either. Could stress throw your body?

The movie was called *Immortal Beloved* and it was about Beethoven's great love. The clouds spun at the end, and the two people remained together swirling and swirling from the vantage point of the sky. Claire kissed Noah.

He said, "It's OK like this, just like this, isn't it?"

Claire said, "Yeah." Her head fit right on Noah's shoulder. Peaceful, she thought. This was enough.

Scrabble and Prayer (Molly)

♦

Noah and Claire had left for the air show. Was that a moth in August? Sure enough it was, escaping from the confines of Molly's closet. Maybe it would turn into a butterfly. No, she remembered, moths only turn into dead moths after they've eaten holes in your good sweaters.

She finished mopping the kitchen floor, a magazine open on the counter to a recipe for mussels. Molly could taste the Penn Cove mussels. It was in Coupeville on Whidbey Island, a damp weekend, when she and Sam had been happy, before the kids were born. A tiny cottage, warm sweaters, coziness.

The phone rang. Molly was startled. It rang again. She hesitated towards it, answered with a question in her voice, "Hello?"

"Molly?" It was Renata.

"Renata," Molly said relieved. She then checked on the cranberry muffins in the oven.

Renata said, "Michael and I are educated; we're professionals. I mean I've seen this kind of thing in divorces I've handled, and even saw what Paul did enlarging that photo when Dorie went to court. I just couldn't imagine something like this happening to me. Molly, he could have taken Jane."

"I know," Molly said, eyeing the darkness of the oven and that lone little light. The day at the JCC still jolted her at times, especially because she didn't know how to stop Renata's husband.

"I'm no different than Dorie. We could have lost our kids, law or no law."

"Is there anything I can do to help?" Molly asked as she shut the oven, put the muffins on the counter, closed her eyes to inhale the homey smell and continued listening.

"You're so there for me. What if Michael tries again? What if he kidnaps the kids?"

"Renata, do you think he will? Can you talk to him?"

"I don't know. Look, I umm called you with some rather disturbing or maybe upsetting news for you."

Molly sat down.

"It's about Arden and I think you ought to know."

"What?"

"He's getting married."

Renata kept talking. She heard it at their monthly meeting about the new library…something else…surprised…she didn't know…but her words were all garbled and marbley as if Molly had plunged underwater.

Molly threw Noah's leather jacket over her summer dress, grabbed her keys and dashed to the car.

The sun was going down as she drove. The trees raced by. Canary palms, California sycamores, pines. Slash, slash, like branches of a tree, detached / detached/. Molly drove on automatic pilot again, doing what she knew she had to do. She became furious, pounding on the steering wheel.

She slammed the car door, didn't show her pass at the reception desk—Miss, your ID, please, can I see your—and banged the automatic door until it beeped open. She marched down the long corridor of the JCC. Someone said "Molly" but it was a blur.

She yanked open the glass door and walked into the light of the pool area. Someone else called something to her—was it Dorie?—but it seemed dim and far away. She threw Noah's jacket on a chair and walked to the diving board. A teenager cut ahead of her.

Christ—it was high. The ladder reached what looked like 12 feet in the air. Sam was there so vividly, and his fist jutted up through the table of glass, punching under her chin, smashing glass everywhere and dislocating her jaw because she had forgotten to go to the dry cleaners. Everything went flying and now danced in the sunlight like dizziness. She turned away, then she quickly recomposed and climbed up. Might as well be now.

She jumped on the edge of the board once—

She turned back. She was too weak. Sam was taunting her.

Twice- It was hard, too hard. Arden laughed mockingly.

Again—

She bit on the pain and turned to leave. The old voice came back. Hell again. Trust again. She had let a man inside her. Fear gripped her breath and the shriek was suffocating. *Do you think of me when you fuck her?* She couldn't live this way anymore.

The second she reached her arms wide to Jesus, she was flooded with a release of serenity. She knew she could do it now.

She jumped.

She went under and it was cool and clear and she reached the bottom fast.

And she sank to the bottom, staying close to it, and then her legs pumped and her arms arced and her dress ruffled the water and she swam. Slowly, then faster, with all the life she had ever relinquished and all the spirit she had ever had. She was swimming again after all these years, getting past everything; she could swim through it. And she swam with one pure breath that held her being in it and she would never let that go. And when she neared the opposite end of the pool—it was possible to reach it, she could see it—she burst through the surface of the water and the blue sloshed over the edge. She gripped the concrete with one hand, gulped a cry and laughed for all the dandelions in the world, for the rapture of one clean breath, for just being alive. She was in the shallow end, the easier part. Christ! She could swim!

She turned in the dusk and there was Dorie, her hands holding the top of her head in a cap of disbelief. She was biting her lip and about a thousand tears flowed down her exquisite face. Molly climbed out, her dress pasted to her.

She could swim again.

The next day, Molly was joyous, radiant. Claire was almost beating her at Scrabble, and Noah was trailing behind. Noah ate some cookies and teased Claire.

"Do you want some tea, Claire? Or more Diet Coke?" Molly asked.

Claire's tiles spelled "under."

Claire eyed Noah. He burst out laughing.

"Coke, please," Claire said.

"You're killing us here. I didn't know you were such a Scrabble champ, Claire. I would've tried harder and been less polite," Molly said.

"Not the dreaded Q," Noah said picking up a tile. "FINA came and did a drug test on Matteo and he flunked."

"Yeah?"

"He's such a dweeb."

"They test for steroids?" Molly asked.

"He'll take anything he can. He's always trying to dress like a gang-banger. Such a loser," Claire said.

"Ever since he didn't make varsity, he's been trying to prove himself," Noah added.

"So, Claire, looks like Virginia has finally given you the car? That's nice." Molly sat down and earned triple points for "quash."

"Finally she lets me drive it. I'm the only 16-year-old at my school who couldn't drive until now."

"Want to help me bake bread?" Molly asked while she popped the can of soda and poured it into a glass for Claire.

"Baking is boring," Noah stated.

"I'd like to learn," Claire said. "Baking is great. You're so good at it."

Noah chose to watch TV.

"I adore you, honey. I want you here," Molly held her elbow when Noah left the room.

Noah watched sports on TV. As they kneaded and rolled the dough, Molly told Claire, "I made your Mama a promise. She called me from Cincinnati and I made her a promise that I'd always...look out for you."

Claire's face paled. Molly wondered if she said too much.

"Mama has no right."

Molly said, "You're such a mature girl. I can't get over it. Not many young women are mature at 16."

Claire rolled her eyes. "No, I'm not." She was embarrassed.

Noah came back in. "I guess I won by default."

"Not so fast," Claire teased.

"More bread? My mother's been baking bread for as long as I can remember." Noah retrieved the milk carton from the refrigerator and let the milk glide down.

"Molly, did your mother teach you how to bake?" Claire asked.

Noah piped in, "No way. We had no money. One time I ate cereal for a snack and she went ape (imitating her): 'That's for breakfast. I can't afford another box.' And then at like 3 in the morning, there was all this commotion and she started baking bread. All night she was in the kitchen baking. My sister thought she had totally lost it."

Molly said, "I had to do something to feed Mariah and Noah. So I started selling bread, then I explored muffins and scones and pies."

Noah said, "It's almost 5:30, Mom. I'll get us a pizza."

"Want a ride?" Claire asked. "I've got Virginia's buggy. I'll drive you."

"Get my purse," Molly said.

But Noah couldn't find it and said, "This one's on me."

The house grew too quiet after they left, but she wanted to see the two of them together. She recognized the tenderness between them. Molly put the kettle on. The phone rang. Molly forgot herself and answered easily. Sam said, "I miss you, Molly. Is that wrong?"

Oh God.

"You don't just throw people away."

Molly slammed the phone down and some seashells smashed to the floor. The phone rang again and then stopped.

She heard a cough outside. But she checked the door, it was locked. She peeked out of her bedroom window. She drew the blinds and the curtains, going room to room.

The kids would be home with the pizza. She had to get control again. Had she left her purse in the car? She bit her knuckle. She had to hurry and get her purse out of the car.

After getting her purse, she realized she had locked herself out.

Damn, damn, damn. She fished under the mat for an extra key. She soiled her finger poking in the flowers and came up empty-handed. She found the key in the saucer under the terra-cotta pot. She didn't remember putting it there. Finally, the lock gave.

She shut the door behind her, leaned against the inside of the door, panting, closed her eyes and prayed. The air was different.

"It's been too long," Sam said. His voice was low and soft and brutal.

"Oh please, oh God."

"Molly, you're always running away from me." He was in the kitchen?

"Sam, no." The tea kettle screamed.

"Why do you keep hiding from me?" He wore a windbreaker and jeans that were too baggy.

"I'm a different person now. I want to forgive you," Molly sobbed. "Please, Sam."

"You took a vow, Molly Wright." He ran his fingers up and down her arm, almost tickling her, but barely.

"I...forgive you. Now leave, now go." She started to run and he grabbed her wrist.

"Come to me, Molly. Come to me."

Whatever he did to her, she had her spirit back.

Embers in the Dark (Claire)

◆

Virginia wore her hot pink baby doll, a mini nightie that left nothing to the imagination and embarrassed Claire to tears. Mama lit up in the grand style. She was propped against some bold orange-flowered pillows in her bed watching yet another boxing match. Virginia decreed it was a hacker's right to smoke where she was most comfy and dang, she earned that right. Claire said, "I'm not arguing with you tonight. Noah and I are getting a pizza and going back to Molly's. Want to come?"

Noah stood in the doorway, at a safe distance.

"That one's a mucker. No class. Look at him, ugly thing." She pointed to a boxer.

"Mama, you sound terrible."

"Get this blanket offa me. I hate blankets. No, sweets, I'm fixin to go to bed early. I just don't feel myself."

"Ya sure? You're not one to miss a party," Claire said. But Virginia passed. When Claire left the bedroom, she didn't see the cigarette that had been dangling in the ashtray fall to the carpet.

The only things Claire would later remember were a police car, flashing lights, a crowd of people and an ambulance or EMS vehicle. Claire had a rock where her stomach used to be. They had been waiting for a lot that summer, but not in a sit-still way. Before this night in August and the day of the Blue Angels and the 21-piece comet band and the sticky Cincinnati nights of July and the nacreous June gloom, there was a sense of something coming. It was spring and something big was taking root, something like love or understanding or the future. This wasn't supposed to happen. Something beyond horror had happened.

Dorie and her sleepy girls, clad in nightgowns, were gathered round. Renata was asking question after question to Jake, the cop. Claire and Noah looked at each other in terror and then Claire said, Oh my God. Oh my God. Claire noticed an ember from a woman's cigarette glow in the dark like a firefly. The woman beside her lit cigarette after cigarette, one in each hand, even offering one to Claire. But Claire didn't move.

Jake spoke to Noah, and Noah howled like an animal. He howled like Claire didn't know what. It was a shriek spinning off canyons. It was a sound that erupted out of space coming from deeper than any music. Worse than a hurling comet of fire. Oh God. He *was* his own hamster blown to smithereens against the wall. Jake turned to Renata, and his words tolled like a bell: they'd get Sam for felony stalking and first—or second-degree murder.

Mama, mama, mama. Claire hugged Virginia. Virginia was a tower of strength, but her mascara was all smeared. "Hold me, Mama. Please hold me."

It wasn't the death foretold by disease and wasting away. It wasn't even the cigarettes to blame. It wasn't a burning house at all. It was burning evil and love gone bad.

Jake put his arm around Renata. She shook her head. It just can't be. Her headband severely held her hair in check.

Dorie, who could be counted on to be defiant, raw and angry, was quiet as a mouse. She didn't want to feel anything. "It's all right, it's all right," she told Natalie and Livie as Molly's body was carted out under a sheet. Dorie's perfect doll eyes wouldn't blink, but would take it all in, would analyze it, would observe the scene dispassionately and then make something out of this nightmare. "Her body…she has her body back. And they say your body is your soul." The girls didn't understand. Neither did Claire.

Claire wondered why they all came around in April and May, Claire and these dazzlers of unmistakable light, gathered around a square of blue. Why did it happen this way? Claire and the finest trio of voices you ever heard in your life. Or, if not the finest voices, at least some of the most gutsy and glorious. Voices of these women, regular women who, when you got to know them, were kind of amazing.

That night, Claire's mama renewed her vow to live. Virginia said, "I have the most important job in the world—bein your mother."

Most of the crowd had dispersed. A man from the coroner's office chewed his gum loudly. "What are you saying, Mama?" Claire was hysterical.

"I don't know," Virginia said. "I'm not fooling around anymore. I've gotta take care of my little girl." Claire wasn't sure if these were the exact words, but she felt the words. Her mama was promising to stay.

The ocean was mysterious, a different color every day, sometimes its tow was muddy green, sometimes it was Crayola blue, sometimes verging on a wave of gray. The pool, well, the pool remained constant turquoise. From house to condo to apartment building, from meet to meet, it never changed. But the deeper you went, the bluer it became. And in that pool, around that pool, everything gave way. Claire learned everything she'd ever need to know about cruelty and friendship and women and giving up and swimming on and how one day you were alive and one day you could wear your heart on your sleeve even if you had no sleeve.

Molly Wright was shot to death by her ex-husband with a Saturday night special. Saturday night special. It sounded like a high school dance or the special of the day at an Italian restaurant. Why didn't Claire recognize the signs? They were there in all the *almosts*! Mama *almost* found another mother for her, then Dorie *almost* lost her kids in court, then Renata *almost* had her kids kidnapped at preschool. Three strikes and you're out. Three *almosts* and then the bad things come. Maybe she didn't notice because she was thinking about Noah and carrying a baby and swimming better than everyone else and taking care of Mama and making music and aiming Robbie's telescope at the stars.

Noah had insisted on going into the house. Jake had told Renata Molly's brains were blown across the floor. Jake tried to stop Noah. He shielded his body in front of the door and said, "She wouldn't want you to see her like—"

But Noah heaved and pushed. Jake pushed him back. "Kid, it's awful in there."

Noah pushed Jake hard, Jake responded in equal measure. Then, Noah punched Jake and knocked him down.

Noah emerged with blood splattered on his white tee shirt. He went wild and had to be sedated. An animal seemed to be grafted on his skin. It was a sad burden.

Claire wanted to crawl into bed under the covers with her Mama and bring Noah with her, but everyone kept her away from Noah. She didn't know where he went.

Late at night, when all the ghosts had gone to sleep, Claire taped Virginia crying in the shower. Then Claire taped silence. Then she put the mike near her mother's face. When Claire returned to her room, she narrated, "Virginia Graham breathing."

Remember Where the Trees (Virginia)

◆

This funeral is different, Claire said. Truly tragic, Virginia hiccoughed a sigh. Claire's plum-forsaken dearest, Noah, what a nice boy, too, read a Yeats or Rilke poem and he squeezed Claire's hand. His sister was home from college and out of control. Virginia just wanted to shake her to stop. Get a hold a yourself, girl! Dorie, having enrolled in a journalism course at San Diego State, moseyed over to Virginia. Years later, Dorie would win an Emmy for a Channel 10 broadcast about domestic violence, and she'd dedicate it to Molly. But the day of the funeral she bit her lower lip clear down to the pulp.

The stone said, "Molly Brown Wright, Always in our Hearts." Her children picked the words. Not that big of a crowd came, but not too shabby either. High atop the hills of the cemetery, Virginia could swear it was Kentucky greens.

When Renata cleared her throat, everyone stopped talkin. She recited Psalm 91:11-12: "For He will order his angels to guard you wherever you go. They will carry you in their hands lest you stumble on a rock." Oh sweet angels. Give her the peace she deserves, Virginia prayed. Renata wanted a grave of flowers for Molly to lay down in and brought a carload of blooms that she tucked in with her hands. Her hands were muddied somethin awful, but she didn't pay no attention. She had the get in her. She was determined in her respect.

Arden looked on, perplexed, like some guilty soldier. Didn't he know every woman wants to be adored? Virginia didn't have a word to say to the scoundrel, not a word.

Claire asked Virginia about safe divin. She was talkin the pool talk again, about goin under, gettin that scaredycat voice. There were little breaks in her confidence that reminded Virginia she wasn't even 17. She was still a kid. But Claire got angry, "No, you're going deaf." Somethin about safe *drivin*. She wanted to *drive* Noah home after the funeral.

Virginia couldn't help but reminisce. She was swimmin the backstroke, somethin she didn't like to do. She had attended more wakes and funerals than weddings in her day. "More folks kickin the bucket than wantin to fuck it," her first boyfriend used to say. She remembered where the trees ended and the Ohio river began in Cincinnati. Remember where the trees...

Renata said trees are sacred, like trees of life. In fact, that reminded her: she was going to have a tree planted in Israel in Molly's name. Yes, that's what she'd do.

Molly wasn't a battered victim, she was a battered survivor, the priest reminded during the eulogy. But she was dead as dirt. She tried to survive, but that gun got in her way. How can he say that? Luckily Virginia knew the songs so she didn't concentrate on the words. Virginia liked "Amazing Grace," one of her favorites. But she didn't care for the poems. Too many poems.

The service over, a woman in black approached Virginia tentatively. Renata complimented Virginia on her beautiful eyes. (Virginia suddenly thought of Milty Harmichael, that one beau, who said her eyes were ever-more blue. Funny how your mind thinks of the darndest things at the darndest times.) Then Renata said, "If only I could be as strong as you are." Renata's collar was perfection and her white shirt properly starched.

Well, Virginia was flustered. Shot out of nowhere too, these kind words. Renata was class, plain and simple. Where Virginia came from, a town too little to cuss a cat in, you recognized that aura. "That woman on the news who gone ahead and birthed sextuplets. Now, *that's* a strong woman," Virginia said. "Good lord, I hope she ain't breastfeedin, though."

Renata smiled easily.

What Virginia didn't mention in good company was if that lady could have that many in one litter, Virginia surely could take care of her one and only little girl. Maybe it was that night that Molly was killed or standing by the police car, watchin them load the body bag. No matter. Virginia decided she just wasn't gonna die.

Dorie hid under her black beret. She was holding back, not spreading her enthusiasm and her mischief around. "You mean he hasn't paid me support and I have to go back to court to collect?"

"Yes, you need to go back to get it enforced," Renata said sadly.

"OK. Then I will." And her anger was replaced with a get-it-done look while her lip puffed up like a jelly roll.

And Dorie, whose little girl played with Renata's daughter so often that she practically became a Meyers child, said thanks and hugged Renata who was like one of them Miss Americas, calm and cool and collected, but not the kind you touch. Virginia guessed Renata ate humble pie after she too almost lost her kids. And she hugged Dorie back, hugged her good.

And then Dorie hugged Virginia. All this huggin! Poor Molly was missin it, that gentle soul. Virginia blew her nose. When Virginia looked at the trees, she wished she could believe Molly just blew away. Natural, like nature. Like a blossom. Virginia shuddered. They couldn't do a good makeup job, so it was closed casket, which made you wonder even more.

"Virginia, it can't be happening like this," Dorie said and circled Virginia's waist.

Virginia usually got excited around Dorie's moxie. Claire said she was too smart and Dorie was the screwy daughter Virginia never had.

Envy if ever Virginia heard it. But it wasn't like that. Goin somewheres with Dorie was like possum huntin with a elephant gun. And Virginia always liked to have fun. She had a soft spot for anyone with gumption. But Claire, well, Claire was her valentine.

"I thought I was next," Virginia admitted. "Molly took my place. It isn't like that entirely, but in some crooked way it is."

"Oh Virginia. You're a fighter. You're going to be kicking around here a long time," Dorie reassured. "I hear you're running for Solana Beach Town Council. Is that true?"

"I sure as Sherlock am."

"But you don't like politics. You told me yourself."

"Speakin of crooked, them politicians are as crooked as a barrel of fish hoo, and I mean it."

"Then why are you running? You can't tell me you're worried about garbage removal or traffic lights?"

"That's beside the point. They have good health insurance, hon."

"Now I get it. Well, in that case, I hope you win."

"Course I will," Virginia said. Maybe if she got whiff of the right politics she could round up all the wife beaters and murderers while she was at it. Have them hanged in front of Jiffy Lube.

Jake arrested Sam, according to Renata, and he was completely unrepentant. As true sinners are. What did they expect? A careful confession? Clean nails on a killer all the way bit down cause he couldn't live with doin wrong?

Dead. Murdered. Gone.

Dorie said, "She felt so much."

Renata said, "It's easier to stand up for principle than to stand up for what you feel. She was brave and I'll miss her." Renata's voice frayed at the edges.

Noah was motherless and the pain on that poor boy's face took your breath away.

In the silence of the whispering trees, you could sense Molly. She was the breeze going through us, Virginia thought.

"I feel her," Dorie cried out loud.

Renata closed her eyes.

Virginia's eyes welled up. Remember where the trees…

Cathedrals in Time (Renata)

◆

The gates to Del Mar Racetrack didn't open until noon that day. Jake misplaced the tickets. He searched pocket to pocket. "Here they are. You think it will be another win like Bertrando's?" The woman at the gate shrugged. The Pacific Classic was a Triple Crown race and attracted the best horses available.

"This is a snazzy one. Only two races in California offer a cool million big ones. This is one of them," he told Renata, grabbing her hand and setting off for their seats.

But Renata didn't remember the 550,000-square-foot grandstand or that this race was a mile and a quarter, a greater distance than the stakes races, or seeing red salvia, yellow marigolds, gray dusty miller and purple ageratum grace the infield tote boards. And she didn't remember the colorful hats or Bing's Celebrity Grill or the guy behind them bragging about Best Pal, "a beautiful gelding owned by my friends, the Mabees," who won the first Pacific Classic. Another woman to their right was betting only on the healthy young 3-year-olds.

What Renata remembered weren't the winning jockeys or how Jake said the ideal gait of a racehorse has a kind of symmetry. Nor did she remember the elegant men with cravats on a crisp summer day or that she wore her favorite white linen jacket. She forgot about the room flanked by photos of Jimmy Durante and Big Crosby. She only recalled Jake's face so purposeful and his words over a few beers, "I'm not going off into the wilderness to pray to some God, Renata. I'm bringing God to my place, bringing Him right here to the track. Right to the table, with us, right now. He says choose life, enjoy all the good things He put on earth. In fact, somewhere in the Talmud it says, you'll be called to task for everything you didn't enjoy. So, naturally, I'm enjoying," and he clinked beer bottles with Renata and downed his hearty drink. Even though Jake lost that day, it didn't alter his mood.

As they searched for where they had parked and the exit, Renata had to laugh. Intelligent people hurt each other with silence and documents. Everyone else says to hell with it and plays the horses.

To be happy. That's what you thought you sought in cobbled streets, exotic cities—Buenos Aires, Avignon, Jerusalem—places where a different language enveloped you, enthralled you, paraded its accented sounds and lulled you by starlight, by bridges, by cathedrals, into believing: far away from your ordinary life, you'd uncover the mystery that makes your life seem whole.

And now Renata sat on a Friday night in a modest temple, its sanctuary lofted with a beautiful high ceiling, decorated with marvelous candelabra and dark wood. She was right at home. Almost whole. A boy played with the fringes on his father's tallit. Who would ever have guessed this would bring her satisfaction?

That didn't mean she wasn't haunted by white nightgowns, the purity of crosses, clean white. "When I first came to San Diego, I was happy there were streets with no snow, but—" Renata said haltingly to Jake. Did she let go of history too easily? Did she let go of her Judaism, her emotions?

"Then what? You missed the snowplows?" Jake teased.

William and Jane said shhhhhh.

Renata was transfixed by the eternal light. The rabbi said shabbat, or the sabbath, is like a cathedral in time. Jews couldn't keep a holy *place*, as they were always forced out of countries and left to wander. So no matter where they were, they could keep a holy *time*. She looked at the light reflecting off the faces of the people around her and someone else's grandparents.

This was a space she could rest in, a place somewhere waiting for her. And yet it was a place that didn't matter much at all because she could take the feeling with her and honor it somewhere else. Shabbat taught her about time and forced her to take time out. It was a modern concept. It was portable, adaptable. She could celebrate it anywhere.

Later, she took the chicken out of the oven. Ready. They stood before the table. Jake suggested, "What do you say we clear the table when we're done and you dance with me, Renata Meyers."

"Soon," she said.

And she remembered Virginia and Dorie dancing on her patio by the pool after Jane's birthday party while she and Molly sat and watched. Molly mustering up courage to tread water. Her discipline and determination. Molly with her hat by the pool, reading as always. The weeping woman with strong hands.

"Renata. Where are you?" Jake asked. He carried the decorative wine cup as the children brought the challah and candlesticks from the counter to the table.

"I'm thinking about Molly." And she allowed herself this. But wait. Why was Jane's lunchbox sitting on the counter? It was not supposed to be there. She had to move it right away. Once she touched it, she ran her fingers down the plastic side edge. Barbie's blonde hair and lipsticked smile stared at her, so she turned the face over. She opened the lunchbox to make sure no surprises were inside. She shook it open over the sink. Crumbs be gone. Every last crumb. She washed the inside.

"What are you doing?" Jake asked. "Let's celebrate Shabbat."

She squirted dishwashing liquid in it. She scrubbed the plastic hard. Then even harder to wipe away all the traces. Every last piece of dirt in the corners.

"Renata, let's do the prayer."

"I have to get it clean," she insisted. She was trying to rub away what she could. All of a sudden, her tongue tingled. A snowflake landed on her tongue. She looked up at her kitchen skylight. The white was coming down.

"Renata."

"Oh my God." She looked at Jakey and back up at the falling white and both her hands flew to her face. She cupped around her mouth to shelter her words. "Oh God. Jakey! He almost took Jane."

"What's wrong with you, Mom?" William said.

There was an implosion so quiet nobody could hear.

"Jane, come over to your mom now."

"No," Jane sensed something strange.

Jake coaxed, "Come, honey. Now, honey. To your mom."

Jake lead her by the hand next to Renata's belly. The little girl's eyes stared into her mother's skirt. Renata gazed at the skylight. "Oh God."

Renata did everything she could to hold her crying back in the cave inside her, but the pressure of the years sluiced out. "Sweet Jane," she cried. And while her daughter leaned against her leg, Renata softly ran her fingers through Jane's dark hair.

"It was a boy," she whispered and sobbed and sobbed.

"Let it, Renata. Just let it." Jake put both arms around her and Jane and his forehead pressed against Renata's.

William said, "Hey, what about me?" He slapped Jake's back and laughed nervously as he joined the Shabbat huddle.

That night at dinner Renata lit the candles and was humbled. She looked at her children. Shadows flickered. Everyone looked beautiful.

She covered her eyes with one hand. *Baruch ata adonai elohenu melech haolam. Asher kidishanu bmitzvatov lehadlik ner shel shabbat.* Jake blessed the bread and the wine next.

Renata then placed her hand on Jane's head and said, "May God make you like Sarah, Rebekah, Rachel and Leah." Maybe ritual was inside of the spiritual. Literally it was one word inside a bigger word.

Then she recited the priestly blessing to her son: "May God make you like Ephraim and like Manasseh." To both she said, "May the Lord bless you and keep you. May He cause his countenance to shine upon you and be gracious unto you. May the Lord grant you peace. Amen." A joyous, bountiful love floated through her. And a peace that was almost whole.

William goosed Jane and they both laughed as they fell into the dining room chairs. Jake's' reverence at that moment touched Renata. He was looking at her kindly and she could feel the heat of his affection. She passed the baked chicken and almond asparagus to him.

A Kiss Good-night (Claire)

◆

Claire used to feel intrepid, that nothing could happen to her or close to her world, as if she was Mama's fly girl.

But things did happen. Mostly out of twisted love. Why? Why?

After the funeral, Claire went to Robbie's house. He was intent on hooking up transmitters in people's mouths so anyone could listen to Nirvana during class. Claire was drawn to the telescope. She'd missed the comet hitting Jupiter. Robbie said, "I couldn't see it anyway." She wouldn't see the blue angels or their maneuvers. She directed the telescope heavenward, toward one star: Molly.

How could she have a baby now?

She used to think that a baby would love her and never leave her. And somewhere waiting for her was the realization that no way in hell could she deal with a child. She could barely deal with her mama. Claire was accepted to UCSD, and school began in a few weeks. She was pre-med even thought Mama didn't cotton to doctors. Mama said she'd get her all the books on the syllabus even if she had to steal them. But Claire had already learned more this summer than any college could ever teach her.

After the funeral, Noah didn't come and didn't call. Mama said let him be, and she showed Claire the photograph of Molly in the newspaper. The paper creased on her soft smile.

Mama munched on carrots with her left hand and inhaled her cig with her right. She said she was eating healthy to live. She turned on another infernal boxing match and asked Claire if she was knocked up. Here Claire knew this woman better than anyone else, but didn't have a clue about how this conversation would go.

"That little tester box has been sittin on your windowsill all summer." Virginia spewed some vile phlegm into a Kleenex. "You crazy girl! How you gonna feed it? Go take the test before I start cussin and gettin too lively. Then come over on the sofa and watch the match while the results cook. This is the fight Randall wins."

Claire shivered with nervousness when she shut the bathroom door.

While the results took hold, she watched those greasers bash each other's face in.

"Go, JC," Virginia yelled. The announcer said Chavez had a record-winning streak and this would be his 90th win if he did win.

"Gross."

Mama said, "Here it is, the eleventh round where Randall puts Chavez down for a count of eight."

"You memorized this?"

"He takes a 12 round points decision."

"I thought you always cheered the Chavez guy."

"I do, but this is an excitin defeat. That's why I got it on tape. Now, hush."

She and Noah only did it once. But she hadn't gotten her period since and she felt so dizzy in Cincinnati, so queasy a lot of the time. Sometimes she felt normal, whatever that was.

"Damn you, Claire. I can't even take care of us right now with no full-time job and no insurance." Mama's eyes became glassy.

Wouldn't Mama rather pay for a getaway to the Bahamas than a pile of textbooks for her? What else had Mama given up for Claire's sake?

The scientist part of Claire said she wasn't pregnant; the musician part said she was. She was heading back to the bathroom to check the results when the doorbell rang.

When Claire saw Noah's face, she felt that loving ache. Mama invited him in and he said, "I let her down. I should've stayed with her."

Mama promptly turned off the taped fight, touched Noah's shoulder and said, "No, honey. You were a good son to that woman. I'll let you two alone." Virginia quietly padded to her bedroom in her pink fuzzy slippers.

"I didn't get the gun in time. I should have had a gun to give her! Or I should have used it. I should have."

"Noah..."

"Maybe I couldn't've stopped Fate, but I could have stopped that son of a bitch." Noah's veins popped in his neck with the heat of his rage. Claire comforted him as best she could.

"What if I couldn't shoot it? What if I got it and couldn't shoot or I froze?"

Claire wouldn't cry, she wouldn't.

"My mother is dead and yours is dying. I need you, Claire. You're the only one who can understand this. She had Post-its all over her room."

"What do you mean?" Claire asked.

"Post-its of little poems."

Claire kissed his eyes. *Stay.* "Do you want to stay? Or how about, let's go out somewhere? I'll take Virginia's soupcan Mercedes. Let's get some french fries."

"No, I can't. Only you can understand." He cried openly.

"Yeah—."

"My sister, Mariah, has to go back to college. I'm going to Santa Barbara with her. I'll start college there. Renata is helping us with the house, the bills, the paperwork. I'm probably moving in with relatives."

Then he got cool again, arranged his feelings into a compartment, fussed with his jacket and prepared to leave. "I've got to go. We're back together, Claire. Right?"

"Yes, we're together. But are you just leaving me like this, just going?"

"No—I've just got to get settled."

He gently kissed her good-night. And he was gone.

Mama sat down and pleaded, "You're too young to have a child. It's way too hard. Maybe you're not too young, but it's too hard right now." The room was smoky. The sound of the bashes and the bells emanated from the TV again. "Claire, you're still a kid yourself. Wait, he's up. He's up Claire. Look at this."

Claire returned from the bathroom. "It's clear, Mama."

"What's that mean?"

"I'm not pregnant."

"Sweet Jesus," Virginia exhaled and clapped her hands softly.

That evening Mama made Claire her favorite dinner. Meaning she didn't cook. She picked up Kentucky fried chicken with mashed potatoes, biscuits and that good coleslaw.

Why celebrate nothing? Maybe the color of nothing is OK. Maybe it holds whatever you want it to hold. Maybe in that space, in that clear path, you are able to breathe, grow.

"Life is gonna knock you black and blue and twist you and turn you round. That's all right. You get up, you fight, you keep on, Claire. Just so long as it don't leave you facin backward. Know what I'm saying?"

"No," Claire said to get her mad.

"I'm sayin turn yourself around. We gonna be all right."

The rock in Claire's stomach disappeared. She felt lighter.

And while Claire ate, while Virginia scooted off into the bedroom, hacking up some furballs, looking for her misplaced medicine, Claire noticed a pile of mail on the counter. Mama usually kept her counter tidy and put the bills in the toaster oven. God forbid you tried to make toast!

It wasn't mail but a stack of birthday cards, probably from Pay-Less. Some were funny, some had line drawings of career women, some were flowery, one Far Side. They were addressed to Claire and most were signed. She was in the middle of writing "Love, Mam—" on one. They were cards from Virginia Graham for every year Claire would be left without a violent boxing match sounding from the TV, without smoke polluting the house, without that annoying, raspy cough.

Cards to keep her company.

Claire pretended she didn't see them and sat on the couch. She was filled up with love. They watched regular TV for awhile. Virginia was tired.

"Good-night, sweets," Virginia said heading to bed. Then she stopped. She scrunched up her shoulders, took a deep breath and with two hands blew Claire a kiss that made a smacking hmmmm-waaaah-hhh sound.

It was a sweet sound. Claire wished she had taped the sweetness of it.